"Jillian? Is this Jillian Gardner?"

The male voice had a familiar cadence, but no one had called her Jillian since she was a kid. "Who is this?"

"This is Cameron Lane. I knew you when you were Harvey and Alice Nelson's foster child."

Cam Lane? The four chocolate sandwich cookies Jilly had just eaten chose that moment to do a square dance in her stomach. His mention of the Nelsons, however, had her struggling to keep her voice even. "I remember. You used to hang out at the inn."

"I know this call is coming out of nowhere, but Harvey asked me to get in touch with you. Alice is in the hospital, scheduled for quadruple bypass day after tomorrow."

Jilly squeezed her eyes shut. She didn't want to care, but she couldn't help herself. If only the past didn't still hurt so much.

MYRA JOHNSON has roots that go deep into Texas soil, but she's proud to be a new Oklahoman. Myra and her husband have two married daughters and five grandchildren. Empty nesters now, they share their home with two loveable dogs and a snobby parakeet. *Autumn Rains*, Myra's first novel for Heartsong Presents, won the 2005 RWA Golden Heart for Best Inspirational Romance Manuscript.

Books by Myra Johnson

HEARTSONG PRESENTS
HP873—Autumn Rains
HP886—Romance by the Book

Where the Dogwoods Bloom

Myra Johnson

Heartsong Presents

'or Mary Conneály, with gratitude for your friendship and inspiration. You're the reason this book exists!

Many thanks to my critique partner, Carla Stewart, for keeping me on track with both her writing advice and nursing experience, and also to law enforcement professional and author Steven Hunt for letting me pick his brain about police procedure. Any errors are my own.

And, as always, I pray a special blessing upon my husband and our gorgeous daughters, the best cheerleaders a writer could have!

A note from the Author:
I love to hear from my readers! You may correspond with me by writing:

Myra Johnson
Author Relations
PO Box 721
Uhrichsville, OH 44683

ISBN 978-1-60260-910-5

WHERE THE DOGWOODS BLOOM

Our mission is to publish and distribute inspirational products offering exceptional value and biblical encouragement to the masses.

PRINTED IN THE U.S.A.

one

"Broken! It can't be broken." Jilly Gardner squinted toward the light box where three X-rays of her left ankle glowed in haunting shades of gray. "Take another look, Doc. Maybe it's just a smudge on your glasses."

"I know what I'm looking at, Miss Gardner." The petite ER doctor's tone sizzled.

Okay, maybe she'd insulted the woman's intelligence a teensy bit. Besides, the doctor's bloodshot eyes and stooped shoulders suggested she'd been on duty all night. "Sorry. It's just . . . this is horrible timing. Are you absolutely positive?"

"Your X-rays clearly indicate a lateral malleolus fracture. Not bad enough to require surgery, but you'll be in a cast with limited weight bearing on that leg for a full six weeks."

Jilly winced as she scooted to the edge of the exam table. She refused to look down at the lower limb swollen to nearly twice its size. "But I've got bills to pay. I can't work with a broken ankle."

"Why not? You drive a standard?" The doctor scribbled something on a chart.

"What does my car have to do with anyth—Ow!" Standing up? Big mistake. She jerked the injured leg toward her chest and chomped down on the inside of her lip.

The doctor scowled over her wire rims. "Not a good idea to put weight on that foot."

"Yeah, I get that." Jilly eased back to the center of the table and allowed a nurse in lollypop-print scrubs to arrange an ice pack around her ankle. She squeezed her eyes shut, forcing out the tears that had begun to pool. *Oh God, this cannot be happening. Not now.*

"Hang in there, Miss Gardner. You're young and fit. It's not the end of the world."

With a loud sniff, she shot her gaze toward the ceiling. A deluge threatened behind her eyes. "I just hope it's not the end of my career."

She ignored the cynical voice in her head that taunted, *What career?*

The nurse patted her arm. "You'll get used to the crutches in no time."

Yeah, right. Kind of hard to swing a tennis racquet while balancing on one foot and two skinny aluminum sticks. Not exactly the perfect summer season Jilly had counted on.

Two hours later, she reclined on the sofa in her garage apartment, the ankle swathed in an ice pack and propped up on pillows. The swelling should go down in a couple of days, and she had an appointment with an orthopedist Monday afternoon to get a cast. In the meantime, pain pills had taken the edge off, and Jilly's world was mellowing fast.

"You need anything else, sweetie?" Her landlady, Denise Moran, set a tall glass of diet cola on the coffee table next to the current issue of *Tennis*.

"Just a new ankle." Jilly scraped a hank of straight, limp hair off her forehead. She desperately needed a shower and shampoo. Not gonna happen today. "Thanks for helping me home from the ER."

"After all you did for me when I had the flu last winter, it's the least I can do." The sixty-something widow plopped down in a Danish-style recliner. "Okay, young lady, tell me how in the world you managed to break your ankle."

"It was freaky. Totally freaky." Jilly poked around in her benumbed brain, trying to put the pieces together. One minute she'd been on a stepladder in the pro shop, retrieving the Becker 11 an adolescent Andy Roddick-wannabe insisted on trying out. She could have told him he wasn't ready for such a high-caliber racquet, but no. It was the Becker or nothing.

Then something in the air tickled her nose—probably the cheap aftershave the kid had slapped on after his shower. Scents and Jilly did not get along. She'd sneezed violently. The stepladder shook and she lost her balance. Then somehow a display of tennis balls got knocked to the floor, and her left foot came down hard on one of the canisters. The ankle gave a violent twist, and she'd yelped in agony.

If she didn't know better, she'd think . . . No, it was her stupid allergies, not an evil plot by an overachiever kid. Acne-faced, outgrowing his own skin, morning breath that could knock an elephant off its feet. And too cocky for his own good. Several of Paul Edgar's students had attitude problems—as did Paul himself these days. Despite her long-standing friendship with the other tennis pro at Modesto's new Silverheels Country Club, Jilly and her girls usually kept their distance.

"Freaky how, honey?" Denise patted Jilly's uninjured leg.

Oops, must have zoned out for a few seconds. Jilly reached for her cola. "I fell off a stepladder when I sneezed."

"They say accidents are most likely to happen when we're doing something ordinary. My mother fell and cracked her pelvis getting out of the bathtub last year. She's in her eighties, so it was quite a scare. You're young, though. You'll heal quickly."

"So I'm told."

But it wouldn't be soon enough. This summer might be her last chance ever to qualify for a major tournament, and now she faced weeks off the competition circuit. A long swallow of ice-cold diet cola did little to soothe the resentment burning the back side of her sternum. *Young* was a relative term in professional tennis, and at twenty-seven, she was way too close to being "over the hill."

❧

Cameron Lane stepped out of his Mercury Mariner hybrid and inhaled the clean scent of country air seasoned with a hint of wood smoke. Gray wisps curled skyward from the stone chimney atop rustic Dogwood Blossom Inn. It was a quiet

Tuesday afternoon, a bit cool for this time of year. Tourist season hadn't officially kicked off yet, so the gravel parking area stood empty, save for Cam's SUV and a four-door Chevy pickup. Probably the Nelsons', who owned the inn.

It would be good to see Harvey and Alice again. He hadn't visited them nearly often enough since accepting the teaching position at Rehoboth Bible College four years ago. Creating lesson plans and grading papers didn't leave much time for keeping up with old friends. A mistake he hoped to correct this summer.

Along with a few others.

His chest throbbed with the sudden urgency to wrap his friends and mentors in a bear hug. He slammed the door of his SUV and took the split-log steps two at a time. He burst in the front door, his mouth stretching into a boyish grin.

The empty lobby squelched his eagerness. "Harvey? Alice? You around?"

Silence.

Must be working out back. They always had plenty to do before the onslaught of summer guests. Cam marched to the tall glass doors that opened upon an expansive view of Missouri's Lake of the Ozarks. The meandering lake stretched one lazy arm along the northeast edge of the Nelsons' property. How many summers had Cam spent casting his fishing pole alongside Harvey's from the little green boat that now lay upside down next to the weathered dock?

He stepped onto the redwood deck. "Harvey! Anybody home?"

A man's steel-gray head appeared in the doorway of a storage building next to the garage. "Glory be! Cameron Lane, is that you?"

"In the flesh." Cam bounded down the steps and met his old friend on the sloping lawn. Their chests thumped together in a manly hug that lifted Cam off his feet.

"Man, you are a welcome sight indeed." Harvey pounded

Cam on the back with one hand while brushing something off his face with the other. A tear? Cam felt his own eyes well up.

"It's been way too long, Harvey. How are you? How's Alice? Is she around?"

The man's face clouded. He took a half step backward and shoved his hands into the pockets of his khaki work pants. "Alice is in the hospital. I was just wrapping some stuff up here, so I could pack a few things and stay in town with her."

Cam's stomach clenched. "What happened?"

"Some heart blockage, looks like. She's been ailing for a while, but you know Alice. Never one to burden others. Took us both by surprise when her cardiologist said she needed a quadruple bypass. The surgery's day after tomorrow."

"Sounds serious."

"Nothin' the good Lord can't handle." Harvey steered Cam toward the inn. "Come on inside and I'll fix us some coffee. Then you can catch me up on what all you've been up to. You'll come with me to the hospital, won't you?"

"Sure, Harvey. You bet."

Two cups of Harvey's stand-a-spoon-in-it coffee later, Cam aimed his SUV back the way he'd come. Concerned by Harvey's pallor and the deepening lines around his eyes, Cam had offered to drive him to the hospital. The old man could be headed for a heart attack himself if he didn't ease up.

"You never said what brought you up to Dogwood Blossom," Harvey said as Cam slowed to take a curve.

"I'm taking a break from teaching—a six-month sabbatical."

Harvey shot him an appreciative grin. "And you decided to spend some time with me and Alice?"

"That's part of it." The rest of his summer plans didn't seem so feasible now.

"I hear a 'but' in there somewhere. What else is going on?"

Leave it to Harvey. He could always read Cam like a large-print paperback. "As part of my sabbatical, I'm hosting a series of weekend prayer retreats for my church. I'd hoped to bring the groups up to the inn. But with Alice in the hospital—"

"No, it's fine. We've already got a good number of regulars coming back this summer, so I gotta keep the inn open. Can't afford not to, what with hospital bills piling up." Harvey sighed and let his head fall against the headrest. "God'll work things out, just like He always does."

Faith like a mustard seed? Harvey had faith like the Rock of Gibraltar. Cam's chest tightened. His own faith was in dire need of recharging. So how exactly had he expected to teach and inspire a bunch of church members on the finer points of prayer?

Maybe he should call off the retreats and help Harvey manage the inn instead.

He was about to open his mouth and make the offer when Harvey straightened abruptly. "Why, I know just who to call."

❧

Jilly's tiny apartment over Denise's garage would never qualify as handicapped-accessible. She'd gotten her boot cast yesterday and already lost count of how many times she'd rammed it into a door frame or chair leg. And turning around in the bathroom on crutches? Forget it!

She grew more stir-crazy every day, but the mere thought of trying to negotiate the stairs tied her stomach in knots. Denise had been kind enough to drive her to the orthopedist and also picked up some groceries and prepared a few meals, but if Jilly had to listen to much more of the dear lady's incessant chatter, her head would explode.

Work. She needed to work. And teaching tennis, the only thing she felt qualified to do, she couldn't. The pro shop manager said he'd try to work in a few shifts for her behind the counter, but he already had a full staff. Even if Jilly could manage coaching her advanced students from the sidelines, the beginning and intermediate players needed demonstrations and hands-on instruction. One or two of her advanced kids might be willing to help, except the ones she'd consider asking had already told her they had summer jobs lined up to help pay for their lessons.

A ragged groan tore through Jilly's chest. *God, are You up there? This is so not fair!*

As she balanced on one crutch to retrieve the milk jug from the refrigerator, the phone rang. She set the jug back in the fridge and hopped on her right foot over to the counter. The caller ID registered a Missouri area code but no name. She couldn't think of a single person in Missouri she'd ever want to talk to again. Warily she lifted the receiver. "Hello?"

"Jillian? Is this Jillian Gardner?"

The male voice had a familiar cadence, but no one had called her Jillian since she was a kid. "Who is this?"

"This is Cameron Lane. I knew you when you were Harvey and Alice Nelson's foster child."

Cam Lane? The four chocolate sandwich cookies Jilly had just eaten chose that moment to do a square dance in her stomach. His mention of the Nelsons, however, had her struggling to keep her voice even. "I remember. You used to hang out at the inn."

"I know this call is coming out of nowhere, but Harvey asked me to get in touch with you. Alice is in the hospital, scheduled for quadruple bypass day after tomorrow."

Jilly squeezed her eyes shut. She didn't want to care, but she couldn't help herself. If only the past didn't still hurt so much. "I'm sorry. I'll send a card or something."

"Actually, Harvey was hoping for some help."

"Help? I don't understand."

"He'll have his hands full taking care of Alice while she recovers. He needs someone to manage the inn for several weeks this summer."

"And that involves me how?" *Please don't ask me what I think you're asking.*

"According to Harvey, you know almost as much about running the inn as he and Alice. He said you pretty much ook over the summer they won that Alaskan cruise and were gone for two weeks."

"I was barely seventeen. And I had a lot of help from the staff."

Cameron chuckled. "You might remember, the staff back then was already ancient. Harvey's current staff hasn't been there long enough to know the inn business like you do. Besides, he really needs someone he trusts, someone who cares about the inn as much as he and Alice."

She may have a few fond memories of her years at Dogwood Blossom Inn, but still. . . "Did it ever occur to Harvey that I already have a job?" *Sort of.*

The line went silent for several seconds. "I guess not. I'll let Harvey know you're not available. He'll understand."

A torrent of emotions churned beneath Jilly's heart. She pictured Harvey's tender, compassionate gaze, Alice's bubbly smile. A part of her still loved that sweet couple, the ones who'd opened their hearts and home to her after she'd worn out her welcome with at least four previous families. The Nelsons were her last foster parents.

She'd hoped for something more. They'd promised more.

It hadn't happened.

"I won't keep you, then," Cameron said. "I'll tell Harvey—"

"Wait." The air rushed from Jilly's lungs. "I'm kind of on leave from my job. I could help for a while, I guess."

"Are you sure?"

Why not? Managing the inn might be just the thing to distract her from everything she'd be missing out on if she stayed in Modesto for the summer. "One small problem. The reason I'm free right now is because I broke my ankle. I'd have to delegate a lot of the physical work."

"Sorry about the ankle, but the staff will be there to help. Harvey just needs someone to oversee things and manage the office. I'll be staying at the inn off and on, myself, so you can put me to work any way you need to."

"Great."

"Harvey will be thrilled. Alice, too."

"Okay, I'll let you know as soon as I've made arrangements." After jotting down his number, she said good-bye, then crumpled against the kitchen counter, jamming her bent left knee against the lower cupboard door.

Great timing, God. If this was Your plan all along with this ankle thing, all I can say is, "You have a weird sense of humor. Notice I'm not laughing."

Though they'd kept in touch with Christmas and birthday cards, Jilly hadn't seen Harvey and Alice since they hugged her good-bye at the Kansas City airport the day she left for Stanford University, nearly a decade ago. Excuses, always excuses. At college it was a test to cram for, a research paper to complete, tennis practice and tournaments. After graduation came the competition circuit, training camps, her coaching schedule.

She should forgive the Nelsons, try to understand.

Maybe in another ten years.

She'd almost decided to call Cameron back and tell him she'd changed her mind when the phone jangled again. Startled, she staggered backward and would have landed on her rear if her kitchen had been any wider and the fridge hadn't broken her fall.

Catching her breath along with her balance, she glanced at the caller ID. Anonymous. Probably a telemarketer. She lifted the receiver and prepared to give her usual brush-off.

Before she could even say hello, static filled her ear, then a rasping voice: "Better forget what you saw, or next time it could be worse." The line went dead.

A *threat?* Jilly's chest felt like it had been hit with a backhand smash. Her pulse accelerated well past training rate, and she hadn't even broken a sweat.

two

"Cam, honey, are you still at the hospital? It's Friday. Did you forget we have dinner plans?"

"Aw, man. I'm sorry, Liz." Cam stood in the parking lot outside Blossom Hills General, cell phone pressed to his ear, right hip braced against the fender of his Mariner. A playful May breeze tossed a scrap of paper across the toe of his sneaker. "I have to pick up someone at the Kansas City airport and drive her up to Dogwood Blossom Inn."

"Her?" Liz's voice took on a suspicious edge.

"Harvey and Alice Nelson's former foster child. She's coming to manage the inn for a few weeks."

"But you'll be back in town for Sammy's ball game tomorrow morning, won't you? He'll be heartbroken if you aren't there."

The image of Liz MacIntosh's wide-eyed eight-year-old son tugged at Cam's heart. So much like Terrance at that age. Innocent. Trusting. Full of big-boy dreams.

He scrubbed a hand over his eyes and wrestled his thoughts back to the present. "You know I wouldn't miss Sammy's game for anything. See you in the morning, okay?"

He pressed the END button and checked the time. If he left right now, he should arrive at the Kansas City airport around the time Jillian—make that Jilly, at her insistence—retrieved her luggage from the baggage carousel.

Heading north toward I-70, he hoped he'd recognize Jillian Gardner after all these years. He still pictured a lanky kid with a thick, coffee-brown ponytail. All arms and legs, and a spitfire temper that matched her skill on the tennis court. The last of the Nelsons' dozen or more foster children to grow up and leave their nurturing home, she was the one they talked about—and clearly missed—the most. Harvey and Alice deserved sainthood for all they'd done for Jilly. He only hoped she appreciated it.

But considering the distance she'd put between herself and the Nelsons, he had to wonder. Not that he'd been much better about visiting, and he lived less than twenty-five miles from his friends. He owed Harvey and Alice an equal amount of gratitude for helping him through the most painful time of his life, a time when his parents were too wrapped up in their own grief to even acknowledge his existence.

"Enough, Lane." He slapped the steering wheel with an open palm and focused on the freeway signs. Time to let go of the past and move on.

ð

You've got to let go of the past, Jilly Gardner.

And good luck with that. The past was about to confront her with all the power of a Venus Williams serve.

As she eased the bulky blue boot cast to a more comfortable position under the seat in front of her, the flight attendant announced over the speaker that they were beginning their final descent into Kansas City. A confusing mixture of dread and homesickness tied knots around Jilly's chest. She pressed her forehead against the cool window and gazed toward the far eastern horizon. She imagined she could make out the nearest arms of the sprawling Lake of the Ozarks as it coiled around the hills like a multi-limbed dragon. If she could only see far enough, she might even glimpse the ribbon of road leading to Dogwood Blossom Inn.

It was a road she once vowed never to travel again. A road that would lead her back to the closest thing to a real home she'd ever known, into the arms of the couple who'd destroyed that dream forever.

Get over it, Jilly. What's done is done, and there's no going back.

The plane shuddered through a burst of turbulence. Nausea threatening, Jilly turned away from the window and fixed her gaze on the lavatory sign at the far end of the aisle. Too late to leave her seat. A red *X* slashed through the restroom symbol.

A more recent memory nudged aside the queasiness: last Saturday, the corridor outside the country club locker room. After three straight hours of teaching tennis classes during which she'd downed two tall bottles of water, she'd been in a hurry to get to the restroom. Not paying attention, she'd shoved through the men's door before she realized it, obviously interrupting a heated discussion between Paul Edgar and one of his muscle-bound protégés. They both spun around and glared at her, the boy quickly shoving something into the pocket of his warm-up jacket.

Muttering an embarrassed "Excuse me, my mistake," she'd scuttled backward, tugging on the door faster than its hydraulic closer wanted to allow. The urgency that brought her there in the first place hadn't given her time to process what she'd seen inside the men's room.

Then, not even an hour later, the misstep off the ladder and a torturous ride to the ER in the pro shop manager's cramped VW. Preoccupied with her broken ankle and then Cameron Lane's unexpected phone call a few days later, she hadn't given the men's room incident further thought until this moment.

Could it have anything to do with the weird voice on the phone, telling her to forget what she'd seen? After hanging up she'd tried to put the call out of her mind, convincing herself it must have been a wrong number. Now she wasn't so sure.

Although Blossom Hills, Missouri, might not be her first choice of destinations, getting out of Modesto sounded like a better idea all the time.

If she could only figure out what she'd walked in on in the men's room. Drugs? Gambling? Blackmail?

No, despite Paul's moodiness lately, she couldn't believe he'd be involved in anything shady. He was too much of a pro.

When the plane landed twenty minutes later, she'd all but given up trying to figure it out. She retrieved her crutches from the flight attendant and hobbled up the jet bridge. At baggage claim, she chose the least crowded spot around the carousel and tried to figure out how to balance on crutches while snagging a moving fifty-pound suitcase. Sure, she worked out—or at least she had until the accident—but her training didn't include airport gymnastics.

A buzzer sounded, a red light flashed, and the metal luggage monster started spitting out suitcases. Jilly spotted her two battered blue bags tumbling onto the carousel behind a dented cardboard crate. While her suitcases traveled the circuit, she fortified herself with a deep breath, then shifted both crutches to her left side, freeing her right arm. With one less "leg" to stand on, she suddenly felt too wobbly to maneuver.

And there went her luggage.

Frustration gnawed on what was left of the airplane pretzels rumbling around in her stomach. She readjusted her crutches and glanced around in search of a sympathetic face, but most of the other passengers had already claimed their bags and left. If someone didn't come to her rescue soon, she could be watching those two blue suitcases circle the carousel all night long.

Just as they came around again, a muscular arm reached past her. A tall guy with thick, ash-brown hair hefted both pieces from the carousel and plopped them on the floor beside her. "These yours?"

"Thanks. How'd you—" Then Jilly looked up into her rescuer's hazel eyes. "Cam?"

He thrust out his hand. "Hi, Jillian—I mean Jilly. I'd have recognized you anywhere, even without that cast."

She studied the contours of the man's face. Beneath a few worry lines and the merest touch of gray at his temples, she glimpsed the young, lean, and roguishly handsome Cameron Lane she remembered. When she first met him, he'd been a happy-go-lucky fifteen-year-old. A prankster who drew perverse pleasure from tugging on her ponytail or dropping creepy-crawly things down the back of her shirt.

Then a couple of years later, Cam's younger brother died unexpectedly, and Cam had turned quiet, introspective. He and Harvey went on long hikes through the hills or spent hours together on the lake in Harvey's little green fishing boat. By then, Jilly had become too wrapped up in school and tennis lessons to give much thought to the changes in Cam. But as a blossoming young woman she'd definitely missed his attention, annoying as it could be.

A sudden shiver raised gooseflesh on her arms. She felt twelve years old again and wished she still had a ponytail.

"My car's just a short walk. Can you make it?" At Jilly's nod, Cam unzipped the flaps at the top of each suitcase and yanked the handles up. Towing the baggage behind him, he led the way. Jilly struggled to keep up while reminding herself she wasn't a kid anymore.

And neither was Cameron Lane.

But he seemed as quiet as ever as he helped her settle into the passenger seat of his SUV. Just as well. With her thoughts bouncing between her growing suspicions about Paul and his tennis student, her apprehension about seeing Harvey and Alice again, and now these girlish feelings fizzing around in her belly, Jilly had plenty to occupy her mind on the drive to Dogwood Blossom Inn.

❧

Not much of a talker, was she? Just as well. Guilt still plagued Cam for breaking his date with Liz tonight. And he sure didn't want to miss Sammy's game. If everything went okay getting Jilly situated at the inn, he should make it.

A heaving breath sounded from the passenger side. Cam glanced over as Jilly shifted and stretched her left leg. "If you need more room, you can slide the seat back."

"I'm fine. Just haven't gotten used to this cast yet." She turned toward the window.

Several more minutes passed, then another sigh. Cam blew out a long breath of his own. He could at least be polite and try to get reacquainted. "So you're in Modesto now. How do you like California?"

"It was actually pretty good, until. . ." Jilly shrugged and nodded toward her ankle.

Cam angled her a sympathetic smile. He checked his side mirror and pressed his turn signal before changing lanes to pass a pickup pulling a boat trailer. "It sure took a load off Harvey's mind when you agreed to come help at the inn."

Another shrug. "Actually, the timing worked out pretty good for me, too."

"You didn't sound so certain when I called you the other day." In fact, the subdued woman next to him barely resembled the energetic, single-minded adolescent he remembered.

"Let's just say it turned out to be a good time to put some space between me and Silverheels Country Club."

"Problems at work?"

"Wish I knew." Jilly tucked a strand of chin-length hair behind her ear. The ponytail was long gone. "Mind if we change the subject? How's Alice? No complications after the surgery?"

"Not so far. I thought you'd want to stop by and see them at the hospital before we head up to the inn. We have plenty of time."

His sideways glance caught her left fist curling around the edge of the seat. She stared straight ahead. "I think I'd rather settle in first."

"Sure, if you—" His cell phone chirped. Retrieving it from the center console, he checked the caller ID—Liz. "Excuse me, I should take this." He hooked his headset over his ear and pressed the CONNECT button.

"Hey, hon," came Liz's sultry voice. Country-western music played in the background, barely drowning out the sounds of little boys' laughter. She must be on her way home from picking up Sammy and his friends at school. "I felt bad about being so whiny earlier and just called to apologize. Forgive me?"

"I'm sorry, too. Didn't mean to cut you off, but I had to get to the airport. I'm on my way to the inn with Jilly Gardner."

"Jilly Gardner, the tennis player? *She's* the Nelsons' grown-up foster child?"

Cam cut his eyes toward Jilly. "Yeah, you've heard of her?"

"I used to date one of the guys on the University of Missouri tennis team. I remember seeing her in a few tournaments when Mizzou competed against Stanford. She was really good, the next Steffi Graf, people said. Then she kind of faded away." Liz's car radio snapped off. "What's she up to these days? Is she still single?"

The back of Cam's neck prickled. Liz's jealous side was showing itself again. Not one of her more appealing attributes. "As far as I know. Haven't seen her in ten years or so. We're just catching up."

A pause. "Don't forget, Sammy and I really miss you. I love you, sweetie."

"I. . .miss you, too. Give Sambo a hug for me." He clicked off and tossed the headset onto the console.

Love. Why'd she have to use that word? Like he didn't already feel guilty enough. He cared for Liz, enjoyed her company. And he loved spending time with Sammy. But he couldn't bring himself to commit to anything deeper with Liz than exclusive dating.

And he wasn't entirely sure why. Liz was thoughtful, attractive, attentive. Didn't complain *too* much about the long hours he devoted to his students and class assignments. One thing nagged at him, though. She claimed to be a Christian, but all too frequently she offered up excuses why she couldn't attend church with him. They were out too late the night before. She had a headache. The weather was too rainy/cold/snowy/hot.

At least she didn't mind Cam's taking Sammy to Sunday school. Every minute spent with that little boy nudged a little more of Cam's self-reproach aside.

He stifled a rueful laugh. As if anything could ever make up for failing his brother. Failing his family.

Failing God.

three

Nothing had changed at the inn. Not even Jilly's old room in the family quarters behind the office. High school tennis trophies lined a shelf over her four-poster bed still covered in the pastel-striped quilt Alice had given Jilly for her fourteenth birthday—a big-girl bedspread to replace the Strawberry Shortcake coverlet Jilly had inherited from one of the Nelsons' previous foster kids.

Ice water flowed through her veins. Much as she wanted to hate the Nelsons, she couldn't.

Easing around to take in the rest of the room, Jilly caught the tip of her crutch on a pink fuzzy throw rug. She teetered forward with a gasp at the same moment Cam arrived with her luggage. The suitcases toppled to the hardwood floor, and Cam rushed over to grab Jilly's arm. Moving the crutches out of the way, he helped her onto the side of the bed.

"I'm okay, I'm okay." Grimacing, Jilly waved away his attentions. Shockingly aware of the heat of his touch, she gave a small cough to cover her uneasiness. "Haven't had a lot of practice time on these sticks yet. I warned you I wouldn't be much use."

"And I told you I'd be around to help." Cam retrieved the fallen suitcases and rolled them over to a bench near the bathroom door.

"I don't need babying, okay?" She checked her resentful tone and tried again. "Anyway, I heard your side of that phone call earlier. Sounds like somebody's anxiously waiting for you back in town. Who's Sambo? Your son?"

"Sammy's the son of my. . .friend." Cam's back muscles strained against his polo shirt as he lifted the larger of Jilly's

22

suitcases onto the bench. "And they're not expecting me till tomorrow morning, so I'm at your beck and call. You want me to help you unpack? You can tell me where to put stuff."

The thought of Cameron Lane going through her suitcase, touching her things, sent a crazy shiver up her spine. She reached for the crutches Cam had laid across the foot of the bed. "That's okay, I can take care of it."

And when did her voice turn so squeaky?

Cam must have noticed. He grinned over his shoulder. "Got something in here I shouldn't see?"

"Just. . .undies and such." She stifled a sneeze. Didn't take her Missouri allergies long to find her. As if she didn't have enough to deal with. She'd better jot herself a reminder to refill her prescription soon.

Gingerly she positioned the crutches against her already sore rib cage and stood. "I'm starving. How about we go see what Harvey's got in the kitchen?"

❧

The next morning, Jilly scooted onto the rolling chair behind Harvey's massive oak desk and propped her crutches against the credenza. Time to catch up on what had been happening at the inn over the past ten years. . .and, more important, what Harvey had lined up for the summer. Last evening, Cam had introduced Jilly to perky, spaghetti-thin Heather McNealy, the Nelsons' new cook, who'd whipped up an amazing five-course meal for them. Earlier today she'd met Ralph Davenport, the retired Kansas City bus driver Harvey had hired as part-time groundskeeper and handyman.

After helping Jilly get settled, Cam had stayed the night in one of the guest rooms. He'd joined her for Heather's gourmet breakfast of whole-wheat french toast stuffed with cream cheese and strawberries and then hit the road. He explained he needed to stop by the hospital with a few items Harvey had asked for before meeting his friend Liz for her son's baseball game. He promised to return on Wednesday, and in the meantime Jilly could call on Ralph, Heather, or one of the housekeepers if she needed help.

She fingered Cam's notes about the weekend prayer retreats he'd scheduled. The first one began next Thursday evening, with six couples in attendance. They'd need seven guest rooms in all, plus the small second-floor conference room overlooking the lake. Three meals a day, coffee break setups, an evening snack bar.

Sounded easy enough—especially after sampling Heather's cuisine. With culinary talents to rival any New York chef, why the girl chose to work at such an out-of-the-way location blew Jilly's mind.

The desk phone jangled. She punched the blinking button and lifted the receiver. "Dogwood Blossom Inn."

"Jillian." Harvey's raspy baritone, rich with emotion. "Hi, sweetheart, how are you?"

Her heart played marimba on the inside of her rib cage. "Hi, Harvey."

"Meant to check on you last night, but Alice had a minor setback, and I got a bit distracted. You settle in okay?"

"Everything's fine here." She swallowed, squeezed her eyes shut. "Just like I remembered."

"Good, good. Cam's here. Says you met Heather and Ralph. They'll take good care of you till I can break away from the hospital."

Jilly fingered the phone cord. "How's Alice this morning?"

"She's having atrial fibrillation. They're keeping a close eye on her, trying to get her heart rhythm to—what did they call it? Convert. Say a few prayers, will you?"

"Sure." If she could remember how. *God, help!* and *Why me?* seemed the best she could do these days.

Silence stretched between them. "Honey, I can't tell you how much it means that you came. But it's like the good Lord whispered your name in my ear. I'm hoping once Alice is better, we can all be together again. Make up for lost time.

We've missed you something fierce."

"I. . .um. . .Harvey, I'm going over the reservations schedule and need to ask you some questions."

❧

Cam kissed Alice's forehead and signaled to Harvey he needed to go. On his way to the parking lot, he recalled Jilly's sudden stiffening when he'd suggested stopping at the hospital. What had caused Jilly's coolness toward the Nelsons? Couldn't be anything they'd done. Harvey and Alice had to be the sweetest, most caring people Cam had ever known. Whatever had come between them and Jillian Gardner, it had to be something *she'd* done.

And if he ever found out what it was, he'd give her a huge piece of his mind.

In the meantime, he had a ball game to get to.

He arrived at the ballpark as the second inning began. Spotting Liz in the bleachers, he waved and picked his way up the weathered steps.

"Just in time." Liz scooted over to make room. "Sammy's next at bat."

As he edged in beside her, the crowd exploded in an ear-splitting roar and surged to its feet. Cam sprang up to see Sammy toss the bat aside, his short legs propelling him toward first base, then second, all the way to third before the right fielder zinged the ball to the pitcher.

Cam pumped his fist. "All right, Sam!"

"Way to go, Sammy-boy!" Liz gave a piercing whistle, then looped her arm around Cam's neck and pulled him toward her until their lips met in a celebratory kiss.

At least that's all it meant to Cam. Liz returned her attention to the game, shouting encouragement to her son when the next batter hit a line drive that brought Sammy home. Cam found himself staring at Liz's profile, long blond waves sweeping across her shoulder. . .and feeling nothing.

When the game ended, Liz invited Cam to join her and

Sammy and a couple of his teammates for lunch at Riley's Pharmacy—her treat, since she got an employee discount. The old-fashioned drugstore soda fountain served up the best chili dogs in town. Afterward, Liz and Sammy shared a double-fudge banana split while Cam nursed a root beer float.

Liz reached across the table and touched his hand. "You're awfully quiet today. Still worried about Alice?"

"A little, yeah." He stared at the swirls of melted ice cream in his frosty mug.

"Bypass surgery is so common now, it's practically the same as getting your tonsils out. She'll be fine."

Cam gave an irritated snort. "Not quite that simple. Alice isn't out of the woods yet."

"I just meant—"

"Mom, can I go play an arcade game with Elliot?" Sammy scooted out of the booth.

Liz rolled her eyes and reached for her purse. After digging around in her wallet, she brought her hands out empty. "Oops, all out of quarters."

Cam fished a handful of change from his pocket. "Here, I've got a few. Knock yourselves out."

"You spoil him." Liz flicked a straw wrapper across the table toward Cam.

Grinning, he flicked it right back. "I love him."

"I know you do. I wish. . ."

A boulder settled atop his chest. His breath hitched. Easy to say he loved that feisty little guy who reminded him so much of Terrance at that age. Why couldn't Cam love Sammy's mother?

He finished off his float and stuffed his napkin into the empty mug. "I should go. Still have some prep work to finish before my first prayer retreat. I'm leading an introductory session during Sunday school hour tomorrow."

"For Pete's sake, Cam, you're supposed to be on sabbatical." Liz sat back with a huff. "I thought we'd get to spend *more* time together, not less."

"A sabbatical isn't just an extended vacation. It's supposed to be a time for reevaluating your life and career, getting a new perspective, learning and growing."

"But why prayer retreats? Why don't you write a book? Go rafting on the Black River? Climb Taum Sauk Mountain?"

"I don't want to write a book, I prefer my water sports in a quiet lake, and I'm not a mountain climber." Cam slid from the booth and fished his keys from his pocket. "I decided to lead the prayer retreats because helping others explore prayer seemed like the best way for me to get closer to God, myself. And that's what I need most right now."

Liz stood and tucked her arms beneath his. "More than this? More than me?"

The warmth of her cheek against his shoulder made him want to do anything but pray. Which meant he needed to more than ever. He eased out of her embrace. "I'll call you later." With a quick good-bye to Sammy, he left.

❧

A blanket of quiet lay over Dogwood Blossom Inn. Jilly roamed the expansive log cabin-style facility, the hardwood floors echoing under her feet—make that *foot*. Step-*thunk*, step-*thunk*. Ralph and Heather had the day off, and since Jilly couldn't stomach the idea of showing up at New Hope Fellowship and facing all the Nelsons' old friends, spending a lazy Sunday at the inn seemed like the best plan.

Years before Jilly came to live with them, the Nelsons had added a small chapel onto the northwest corner of the inn. A peaked roof arched above rows of lacquered pine benches inside the chapel. Floor-to-ceiling windows behind the altar looked out upon stately oaks and hickory trees marching up the hillside, the occasional dogwood peeking through the canopy for a glimpse of sunshine. A few weeks ago the forest would have been awash in white blossoms and the woodsy fragrance of dogwoods.

Jilly had forgotten how soothing this special place could be. She edged onto a bench and let the spectacular view wash over her.

"I'm still not sure about this, God." She allowed her gaze to settle on the hand-carved wooden cross suspended above the altar. "How many times have I told You? I can't forgive Harvey and Alice for letting me down. Is bringing me back here Your way of forcing me to do the impossible?"

All things are possible with God.

"But not with me, Lord. I'm only human."

She sat in silence for a long time, then finally rose with a sigh and headed to the kitchen for a ham sandwich. Spreading mayonnaise across a slice of wheat bread, she decided she'd already been spoiled by Heather's incredible cooking. She'd have to find some way to work out if she expected to stay in shape over the summer.

As she hobbled over to the fridge to put away her sandwich makings, the phone rang. It took another three rings before she could grab the kitchen extension. "Dogwood Blossom Inn. This is Jilly."

"Hi, it's Cam. How's it going?"

Her heart chose that moment to try a syncopated rhythm. She took a second to let it normalize. "Oh, just peachy. Having a sandwich, getting ready to tackle the summer reservations schedule again."

"So no problems, huh? I'm at the hospital. Harvey asked me to call and check."

She stretched her mouth in a phony smile, hoping it would leach into her voice. "Tell him I've got things under control."

"Alice is still in A-fib."

Jilly hunched over, an imaginary eggbeater churning inside her stomach. Surely she could have mustered the compassion to ask about Alice. But no. Self-centered-R-Us. "I'm so sorry. Please tell her I'm praying for her."

And she would. Starting right now.

Cam offered what little he knew about Alice's condition, saying the doctors were monitoring her and that Harvey planned to stay in town until Alice was on the mend. "In the meantime," Cam went on, "I was thinking I'd come on out to the inn this afternoon."

Jilly swiveled toward the window. Out by the lake, the afternoon sun polished the silver-green keel of Harvey's old rowboat. "I thought you weren't coming until midweek."

"Decided I could use a few extra days of peace and quiet to get ready for my first prayer retreat. And Harvey reminded me Ralph and Heather had already asked for the day off, so I could be there to help with whatever you need." A pause. "You don't mind, do you?"

"No, that's fine." There went her crazy heartbeat again.

"Great. See you in a bit."

"Could you maybe pick up a pizza or something? Since Heather's off, I mean."

"You bet. I'll bring a movie, too."

"Great." As Jilly hung up, a shiver of déjà vu rippled up her spine. Pizza, Cam Lane, and *Braveheart*. Even though it was R-rated, many of her school friends had seen it and told her what a fantastic movie it was. Anything with Mel Gibson had to be good, but Jilly had seen the previews and knew she'd never be able to sit through all the blood and guts.

Then one rainy Saturday, Cam got permission from the Nelsons to bring the video up to the inn. Unfortunately, he also brought Terrance, his annoying younger brother, for whom the term *bully* had been coined. Alice stuck two frozen pizzas in the oven, and they all sprawled on the sofas in the lounge to watch the movie on the inn's big-screen TV.

Determined to stick it out, Jilly held her breath and squeezed her eyes shut whenever the scenes became too intense. Terrance kept sticking his pimply face in Jilly's, mimicking a fraidycat whimper and punching her in the shoulder until her arm went numb. Neither Alice's stern glares nor Harvey's quiet warnings had much effect on the boy's behavior.

Finally Cam had come to Jilly's rescue. Without a word, he grabbed Terrance by the scruff of the neck and plunked him down in a chair across the room. Joining Jilly on the sofa, he tucked her under his arm, shielding her eyes during the scary parts and telling her when it was safe to look.

She'd harbored a secret crush on him ever since.

&

Cam placed the pizza order, then stepped next door and browsed the video shop while he waited. What movie would interest a girl like Jilly? He had to keep reminding himself she wasn't a kid anymore. Jillian Gardner was all grown up.

Maybe she'd prefer something athletic, like *Wimbledon*. Or action/adventure—*Indiana Jones* or *Pirates of the Caribbean*. For all he knew, she might be into romantic comedies, but Cam didn't want to go there. Not this weekend.

He decided on *Ratatouille*, a clever animated feature Sammy had enjoyed and Cam wouldn't mind seeing again. If it didn't appeal to her, he'd just excuse himself and settle in with one of the books on prayer he needed to study.

Heading to the checkout counter, Cam took a shortcut and found himself on the aisle displaying classic dramas. A familiar title caught his eye—*Braveheart*—and in the space of a nanosecond his thoughts traveled fourteen years back in time. He forced his mind past the memory of Terrance's misbehavior, actions that should have clued him in from the start.

Instead, he concentrated on the first time he'd noticed—really noticed—the Nelsons' precocious foster child. He could still feel her shivering against his rib cage, still hear her tiny, scared voice: *"Is it over yet? Tell me when I can look."*

When the video ended, she'd released this huge, noisy, lung-collapsing sigh. Knees drawn up to her chest, she smiled up at him and squeezed his hand. Their eyes met for a brief instant before two bright spots of pink flamed on her cheeks.

Abruptly she bolted from the room, swinging that ponytail he took such delight in tugging on.

That was the moment he realized what a beauty Jillian Gardner would grow up to be.

The moment he wished she wasn't four years too young for him.

four

Well, the grown-up Jilly Gardner wasn't too young for him now.

Cam slid the extra-large pepperoni-mushroom-black olive pizza onto the counter, his gaze fixed on the way Jilly's coffee-colored bob formed a comma around her left ear. Balanced on her crutches, she bent over the oven controls. "You think two-fifty is hot enough?"

He cleared his throat. Why did his T-shirt neckband suddenly feel too tight? "That should keep it warm till we're ready to eat."

Jilly pulled open the oven door so Cam could set the pizza box inside. "I saw some colas in the fridge. Help yourself." She hobbled over to the counter, where Cam had laid the DVD. "*Ratatouille*. Fun."

"Seen it?" Cam popped the top on a lemon-lime soda can. Maybe an ice-cold drink would cool him off. He tried to call up an image of Liz in his mind's eye. He should be thinking about her, not the woman who'd brought the Nelsons so much heartache.

"No, but I remember the trailers." She flipped the DVD box over and studied the blurb on the back. "You should have brought that little boy you've been talking about. I bet he'd like this movie."

"Sam. We already watched it together. He loved it."

"Did you make it to his ball game okay?"

"Great game. Sammy's team won by three runs. He even hit a homer in the sixth inning."

"Sounds like he's really special to you." Jilly started for the door, then glanced over her shoulder with a wry grin. "Or is it his mom who's so special?"

Soda fizzed up the back of Cam's throat. For a second he couldn't get any words out. "Liz is just a friend."

"Ooookay." Jilly's wide-eyed stare suggested maybe his response had come out a bit too forcefully. "Keep telling yourself that, big guy." She cut through the dining room and headed toward the lounge.

Cam took another swig of soda, then drew his shirtsleeve across his lips. Maybe he should be using some of his sabbatical time to figure out what he really wanted in a relationship. Liz obviously wanted more than he felt ready to give.

&

Same lounge, same extra-long wraparound sofa. New upholstery, new DVD player, new widescreen HDTV.

And definitely a new and improved Cameron Lane. Her cast cradled by a throw pillow atop the coffee table, Jilly scooted deeper into the brown velour cushions and admired Cam's lean, muscled frame as he set up the DVD. How did a Bible college professor stay in such great physical shape? And she liked the way he smelled. Cologne-free, just a clean, manly scent.

Cam tossed her the remote and dropped onto the sofa beside her. "You're in charge of the TV. I'll be the pizza-and-cola gofer."

"Sounds like a plan." She scrolled through the menu options and pressed PLAY MOVIE. Much safer to watch an animated rat who loved to cook than dwell on long-forgotten feelings for a man who already had a girlfriend and probably couldn't care less about the kid he once rescued from his bullying brother. Besides, Jilly didn't plan to stick around Blossom Hills, Missouri, any longer than necessary.

Half an hour into the movie, she found herself dozing. Her mind flitted through a parade of crazy images—Heather with a rat nose, cooking for a snobby food critic who bore an uncanny resemblance to Mel Gibson. Cam galloping through the inn on a white steed. Terrance the bully's acne-pitted face staring over Paul Edgar's shoulder in the country club men's room.

A tap on the arm stirred her from her dreams. She blinked and tried to focus on the man with the half grin gazing down at her. "Was I asleep?"

"I'd say so. A bit jet-lagged, are we?"

Fists pressed into the sofa cushions, she pushed herself upright and tried to read the numbers on the digital clock over the TV—7:23. "Remember, it's two hours later here. My body's still on California time."

"You'll adjust in a couple of days." Cam chuckled when a loud rumble emanated from somewhere beneath her waist-band. "Sounds like you're ready for some pizza."

While Cam went to the kitchen, Jilly finger-combed her hair and rearranged herself into a somewhat more dignified position. She only hoped she hadn't drooled during her nap. Not exactly Sleeping Beauty material.

The TV displayed a freeze-frame of Remy the rat balanced on the rim of a stockpot. The image sent Jilly's mind spinning back through her jumbled dreams. *Terrance in the Silverheels men's room?* What was *that* all about?

And then it dawned on her. The reason those students of Paul's bugged her so much was because they reminded her of Terrance Lane. Bad attitude, bad complexion, and, oh yeah, even the bad breath.

Cam returned with the pizza box, paper plates, and napkins. "Be back in a sec with the drinks."

"Cam," Jilly called as he turned to go, "tonight got me remembering your brother. I don't know if I ever told you how sorry I was about his death."

He halted in the doorway, his chest collapsing. "Thanks. It's still hard to think about."

"It was the year you graduated from high school, wasn't it?"

"Yep." He straightened. "Better get those drinks."

❧

In the kitchen, Cam stalled long enough to lean over the sink and splash water on his face. Why did Jilly have to bring up

Terrance tonight? As if Cam's mind didn't dwell on the tragedy every waking moment of his life since the day his mother found her second son collapsed in the basement next to the weight machine.

At the sound of Jilly's crutches creaking through the dining room, Cam snatched a paper towel from the roll by the sink and blotted his face. By the time she entered the kitchen, he'd tossed the towel in the trash and had filled two tumblers with ice.

He shot a forced grin over his shoulder. "What are you doing up? You're useless in here, remember?"

"I needed to stretch." She pursed her lips. "And I wanted to apologize if bringing up Terrance upset you."

"Forget it." Cam opened the refrigerator and tried not to think about the pitying stare she must be leveling at his back just now. "Cola? Lemon-lime? Root beer? Name your poison."

"Better make it something with caffeine, or I'll never get through the rest of the movie."

"Cola it is." Cam tucked two cans under his arm and grabbed the tumblers off the counter. He glared at Jilly and nodded toward the door. "Get a move on, girl, before my armpit goes numb."

She rolled her eyes. "Try crutches for a few days, and you'll come to appreciate numb armpits."

A welcome lightness warmed Cam's chest. This was the Jillian Gardner he'd always liked best. Spunky, sassy, spirited. He'd focus on those qualities instead of the memories her mention of Terrance had dredged up.

Although he might be wiser to keep the grown-up Jilly at arm's length. A few hours in her company and he had the sense she could easily send him careening down the fast track toward an emotional train wreck.

⁓

By Tuesday morning, Jilly had the inn routine firmly in hand. The inn had occasional guests year-round, but the summer season officially launched with Memorial Day weekend, which also happened to be Cam's first prayer retreat. Yesterday she'd gone over menus with Heather and placed the food order with their supplier. The housekeeping staff would resume full-time duty starting Wednesday. Ralph had the grounds looking spiffy and had set aside today to take care of some minor repairs to the boat dock and gazebo.

Seated at Harvey's desk, Jilly gazed out the broad picture window overlooking the lake. To her left, the redwood deck stretched across the back of the inn. She glimpsed Cam reclining in an adirondack chair, a pile of books on a side table and a legal pad propped on one thigh.

A raspy breath slid between her lips. If she'd known how quickly her youthful crush would come rushing back, she might have given more serious thought to her decision to return to Dogwood Blossom Inn. She'd better shake it off in a hurry, though, because the guy was spoken for. As they resumed the movie Sunday night, all Cam would talk about was Liz and her little boy.

Just a friend. Right. "Methinks Mr. Lane doth protest too much."

Rubber soles squeaked on the floorboards outside the office. Heather stepped into the room, her white chef's apron covered in chocolate-brown speckles. She waved a slim silver cell phone. "Hey, Jilly, this yours?"

"Did I leave that in the kitchen again? Sorry."

"No prob." Heather dropped the phone into Jilly's outstretched hand. "It started buzzing. I think you have a voice mail."

"Thanks." Jilly thumbed a key to scroll through recent calls. One from her landlady, Denise. Another from Silverheels Country Club. Probably Therese Fessler, her boss.

"Gotta get back to my dessert. A new twist I came up with for buttermilk pie. If you and Cam like it, I'll serve it this weekend."

Groaning, Jilly patted her stomach. "I bet I've already gained five pounds eating your cooking. Soon as I return these calls, I'm headed to the exercise room."

After which she planned to strangle the Dogwood Blossom chef. No one who sampled her own creations with Heather's gusto deserved to stay that skinny.

Alone in the office again, Jilly listened to her messages. The first one was from Denise. "You told me to check your mail for bills. I've forwarded a couple to you."

Bills. Couldn't travel far enough to escape those. She never thought to ask if Harvey planned to pay her for managing the inn. If he offered, fine. If not, at least she was getting a little help from Worker's Comp.

Her nose tickled and she reached for a tissue. Drat these allergies. She had enough pills to last another two or three weeks at most. She'd need to place a refill order soon.

The next message was from Paul. "Hey, Jilly, hope your ankle's okay. Therese said you'd be out of town for a while. She's got me doubling up on classes and working my tail off." A pause. "Give me a call, will ya? Got something to ask you about."

Hmmm. Maybe something to do with that little episode in the men's room?

A third message began. For the first few seconds Jilly heard only static. Then a sandpapery voice: "You talked to the cops, didn't you? Bad idea." *Click.*

"You have no more messages. To save your messages, press—"

With shaking fingers Jilly hit the END button. Talked to the cops? Did the caller mean the nice guy in the Modesto PD uniform who'd helped her into the ER the day she broke her ankle? About all she'd managed to say to him was a pained thank-you.

Clearly, someone believed she knew something and wanted to make sure she didn't tell.

"You look like you ate some bad sushi. Everything okay?"

She looked up to see Cam standing in the doorway. "I'm not sure."

"About the sushi, or about being okay?" He smiled, but concern filled his eyes.

Her shoulders drooped. "How are you in the advice department, professor?"

☙

"So you have no idea what you walked in on." Cam propped his elbows on the deck rail behind him and studied Jilly's face. The usual impish sparkle in her eyes had vanished.

Seated in one of the adirondack chairs, she hugged her rib cage. "Not a clue."

"And you think it has something to do with your accident?"

"It sounds crazy, but yes. The kid I showed the racquet to wasn't the one from the men's room, but I've seen them hanging out together."

"You also had a voice mail from this Paul guy? No indication of what he wanted to talk to you about?"

"Paul's an old friend. If he's involved in something shady"— Jilly shuddered—"I'm almost afraid to find out."

"Call him back. At least find out what he has to say." Cam pulled a chair next to Jilly's. "Put it on speaker. Maybe I can pick up on something."

Casting him a skeptical frown, Jilly tugged her phone from her pocket. She pressed several keys and then hit the SPEAKER button.

"Jilly. I was hoping you'd get back to me."

She glanced at Cam, who gave her a reassuring nod. "Hi, Paul. Got your message. What's up?"

"Thought I should touch base with you before the Memorial Day weekend tournament. I see you have three of your girls entered."

"Oh, man, I forgot all about that. Are you working with them?"

"Yeah, but it's hard to keep up. Like I said, Therese gave me all your students on top of mine." A sharp sigh. "I told her it wasn't a good idea, but she said I didn't have a choice. Silverheels is trying to watch expenses, so they're not hiring a replacement for you while you're on leave."

The guy sounded stressed, but Cam hadn't heard anything to suggest a threat or illegal involvement. Maybe Jilly had an overactive imagination. She'd replayed the last message for him. *"You talked to the cops, didn't you? Bad idea."* Maybe it was just someone on the country club staff who was afraid she'd sue over her accident.

He caught her looking at him, a question mark in her eyes. He shrugged and signaled her to keep talking.

"I appreciate your help with my kids. I know they can learn a lot from you."

"It's just. . .you know my guys. They take the game seriously, both on and off the courts. You've got a good bunch of kids. I wouldn't want there to be any trouble."

Nothing in the man's tone had changed. Cam rolled the words around in his brain, inspecting them for hidden meaning. He cocked an eyebrow at Jilly and shook his head.

She released a controlled breath. "My kids have good heads on their shoulders. They'll be fine. Anything I can tell you to help get them ready for the tournament?"

The conversation turned to things like racquet tension, backhand technique, and other tennis stuff beyond Cam's understanding. When Jilly took the phone off speaker to continue her discussion, he rose and strode to the railing.

If only Terrance had had somebody with a "good head on his shoulders" looking out for him when his athletic ambitions led him down the wrong path. It should have been Cam.

It wasn't.

five

"Here you go, Mr. and Mrs. Hartford. Room 207, top of the stairs, third door on the left." Jilly handed the elderly couple their keys and tried not to inhale. An overpowering gardenia scent played havoc with her sinuses.

Mrs. Hartford leaned on a three-footed cane. "I don't get around like I used to. Do you have an elevator?"

"Just past the stairs and around the corner." Jilly pressed a tissue to her nose. "Need help with your luggage?"

Cam came in from the deck, notebook under his arm. "I'll get it for you, Ruth. How was the drive up, Ivan?"

"Gorgeous. Been looking forward to this retreat ever since we saw it in the church bulletin."

Before Cam and the Hartfords had left the lobby, two more seventy-something couples arrived for the prayer retreat. By five o'clock everyone had checked in. Apparently Cam's first group consisted solely of senior citizens. Jilly decided she'd better remind Heather to go easy on the spices. The inn's selection of emergency toiletries didn't include antacids.

As she came around the front desk on her crutches, Mr. and Mrs. Hartford appeared from the direction of the elevator.

"I declare, you're worse off than I am." Scooting forward with her cane, Mrs. Hartford cast Jilly a sympathetic frown. "What happened, honey?"

"A minor mishap with a stepladder."

Mr. Hartford harrumphed. "Couldn't have been minor with a cast that big. We'll say some prayers for you."

"Thanks." Jilly gave a self-conscious nod. "Dinner will be served in the dining room at six-thirty. Feel free to explore the grounds while you're waiting."

Mrs. Hartford edged closer. At least some of the gardenia scent had dissipated. "I was telling Cameron earlier that you look so familiar. He says you grew up here."

"That's right." The old resentments tied knots in Jilly's stomach. With effort she kept her expression neutral. "The Nelsons were my foster parents."

"Then we should know you," Mr. Hartford said. "We used to attend New Hope Fellowship with the Nelsons before we moved across town."

Jilly shrugged. "I've been away almost ten years."

"You're not. . ." Ivan Hartford squinted. "My word, Ruth, it is! It's little Jillian, the tennis player."

Mrs. Hartford gasped, her mouth spreading into a happy grin. "Jillian, of course! Harvey and Alice were always so proud of you, the daughter they never had. Haven't you grown into a lovely young lady!"

Heat crept up Jilly's neck. She flicked her gaze toward the kitchen and hoped for a quick escape.

"What, and no ring on that finger? Oh, my, and our handsome Cameron being single and all." Mrs. Hartford tugged on her husband's sleeve. "We must get these two together, Ivan."

Please, Lord, get me out of this. "I believe Cam is seeing someone."

He would pick that moment to jog down the stairs—and looking svelte in slim-fitting black jeans and a V-neck cotton pullover with the sleeves pushed up. He sidled between the elderly couple. "Ivan, Ruth. Just the folks I was looking for. Get settled in okay?"

"Room's excellent." Mr. Hartford clapped Cam on the shoulder. "And what a view of the lake."

Mrs. Hartford linked her arm with Cam's. "We were just telling Jillian—"

"She prefers Jilly." Cam winked.

Jilly felt her blush deepen. "I need to get to the kitchen and check on dinner preparations. Will you excuse me?"

She did her best imitation of a graceful pivot on crutches and hurried from the lobby. Good thing Cam's girlfriend wasn't around to see him flirting like that.

Oh, get over yourself, Gardner. Of course Cam wasn't flirting, just being cute for his friends on the retreat.

Which, frankly, caused her even greater chagrin. She'd never be more to him than the gangly youngster with tennis on the brain and a brick where her heart should be.

❧

His back pressed against the rough trunk of a dogwood tree, Cam smiled at the six elderly couples seated in lawn chairs around him. The first morning of the retreat had gone well. "Before we go inside for lunch, I'd like to close our session with a reading from the Psalms."

He thumbed through the pages of his well-worn Bible until he found Psalm 17. " 'I call on you, O God, for you will answer me; give ear to me and hear my prayer. Show the wonder of your great love, you who save by your right hand those who take refuge in you from their foes.'"

Cam's voice trailed off, and he allowed the psalmist's words to resonate in his thoughts. He wanted to believe God heard his prayers. This morning he'd invited the couples to share any personal experiences of answered prayer, and some of their stories bordered on the miraculous. Protection during a restaurant robbery. Healing from a supposedly terminal illness. The birth of a healthy child after they'd been told they could never conceive.

How much of a miracle would it take for Cam to finally have peace?

"Good job, son." Ivan Hartford stood over him, offering a hand up. "This retreat is already filling up my spiritual well."

Cam dusted off the seat of his jeans as he ducked from beneath the tree. The Hartfords, sadly, hadn't received the miracle they'd prayed for. "You've had a tough year, haven't you, Ivan?"

"Not easy losing a child. Ruth took it even harder. Madeline's cancer was the toughest thing we've ever had to face." Ivan released a noisy breath. "Guess your family knows all about loss, though. I remember how broken up your folks were after Terrance died. They sure are blessed to have you."

The old wounds throbbed. Cam's fingers tightened around his Bible. He couldn't say what he really thought. Instead he said, "They've retired to Arizona, you know."

"So we heard. Be sure and give them our best next time you're in touch." Ivan took Ruth's arm and supported her as they followed the other retreat participants into the inn.

On the way through the lobby, Cam stopped at the front desk, where he found Jilly seated on a barstool behind the counter. He leaned across the counter to see Ralph, the groundskeeper, arranging a footrest for Jilly's cast.

Ralph straightened and dusted his hands. "There, that ought to be more comfortable for you."

Jilly tested the footrest. "Much better. Thanks."

Ralph swiveled toward Cam. "Got everything all ready for your evening campfire by the lake. Should be a beautiful night for it."

"Sounds good. Thanks."

Jilly flicked her hair behind her ear, a gesture Cam grew more and more fascinated with. He stared at her earlobe and wondered how it would feel to comb his fingers through the thick hair at her nape.

"Cam? Earth to Cameron." Jilly waved a hand in front of his eyes.

He jerked backward, his face burning. "What?"

"I just asked if everything's going okay with your group."

"Oh. Yeah. Fine."

She nodded toward the dining room. "Better join them for lunch. Heather's serving manicotti and homemade sourdough bread. The marinara is to die for."

"You've eaten already?" Why the thought should fill him

with such disappointment he had no idea. *What is wrong with you, Lane? Jillian Gardner is trouble on two—make that* one *leg.*

Jilly dropped some envelopes into the out-box on the end of the counter. "I ate with Ralph in the kitchen. We needed to talk over some inn business."

Ralph propped an elbow on the counter and tipped his head toward Jilly. "This gal's on top of things. Harvey did good having her come fill in for him."

The hesitant smile curling Jilly's lips drew Cam's gaze. He coaxed his eyes upward to meet the brown ones looking back at him. "I'm glad it's working out."

Ralph shook his head. "You realize this gal hasn't even seen the Nelsons since she got to town? I offered to cover the desk so she could visit them at the hospital, but she won't hear of it."

"Really, it's okay." Jilly waved a hand. "There's too much going on here. I'll have plenty of time to see them next week."

And what excuse would she come up with then? Anger bristled where moments before Cam had once again been fighting the attraction he should rightly be feeling for Liz. What was it about Jilly Gardner that so thoroughly messed with his head?

❧

"You like him, don't you?" Ralph shot Jilly a crooked grin.

"Cam? Please." Ignoring the pinpricks tickling her neck, Jilly straightened a stack of blank registration cards. "He's a nice guy. Like a brother. I'm sure he thinks of me the same way."

Ralph hooted. "Doubt that!"

"You know what I mean. And anyway, he has a girlfriend. Sounds like they're getting serious."

"Liz MacIntosh? Pshaw. Those two are oil and water. Sunshine and rain. Porterhouse and frankfurters."

"You know what they say. Opposites attract." Jilly found a letter opener and sliced open one of the bills that had come in the morning mail. The momentum of her forceful stroke swung the opener within inches of Ralph's chin.

He flinched. "Careful there, girl."

"Sorry!" She dropped the letter opener onto the counter, her fingers darting to her forehead. She smoothed back her hair and groaned. *What is wrong with me?*

"My fault. Got you all riled up with my teasing. Can't help it. You remind me of my granddaughter."

Jilly couldn't resist a smirk. "Oh, and I suppose your granddaughter appreciates Grandpa meddling in her love life."

"Not in the least. But since her dad died a few years ago, I'm her only father figure, so I do my part to make sure she stays on the straight and narrow. Career, love life, whatever." Ralph chuckled. "Meddling is my middle name."

Jilly's throat tightened. She ducked her head and swallowed. "She's lucky to have you."

"I'm lucky to have her. The Lord blessed me mightily when He nudged Heather to return to Blossom Hills."

"Heather? The chef?" Jilly brought her chin up in surprise. "She's your granddaughter?"

"You didn't know?" Ralph furrowed his brow. "But then why would you unless somebody told you? She's never called me Grandpa, always Ralph."

"So Heather's mom is..."

"My daughter. She got a job in Joplin after her husband died. Not long afterward, Heather finished chef's training at this fancy school in Paris. She didn't want to be too far from her mom, so when I learned the Nelsons needed a new cook—excuse me, *chef*—she took the job."

Jilly quirked a brow. "I wondered how someone with her talents wound up in Blossom Hills."

Ralph crossed his forearms atop the counter. "You're a local girl, too. How's it feel to be back?"

"Weird. Very weird." A gnawing sensation scraped across Jilly's stomach. She picked up the bill she'd just opened and studied the figures.

"Well, I know for a fact you're a blessing to Harvey and Alice." He turned to go, then shot her a pointed look over his shoulder. "And you best get yourself into town to see them right quick, or I'll pack you into my pickup and haul you up there myself."

Jilly huffed. Apparently Ralph's meddling didn't stop with Heather. If one more person told her she needed to go see the Nelsons, she'd throw her crutches at him.

six

"You need to go see the Nelsons." Cam leaned in the office doorway, one eye narrowed in an accusatory glare. "The retreat is over. You have three days of quiet before the next group gets here. No more excuses."

Jilly's chest collapsed. Since Harvey couldn't break away from the hospital, Cam had decided to stay at the inn most of the week. Helpful intentions or not, he'd become a major thorn in Jilly's side. Giving a huff, she clicked the PLACE ORDER button on the mail-order pharmacy Web site and turned away from the computer. "You won't give me any peace until I do, will you?"

"Nope." Cam stepped into the room and kicked the door shut behind him. "Whatever you did to create this wall between you and the Nelsons, I know they're more than willing to forgive—"

"*They're* willing to forgive?" Jilly shoved to her feet, wincing when the injured ankle took her weight. She quickly shifted to her right foot and braced one hand on the desk. "I'm the one who needs to do the forgiving. I'm the one who was wronged."

"You?" Cam spread his hands, a confused look etching his face. "You're the one who left. You stayed away for ten long years. Do you have any idea what that did to them, how much they've missed you?"

"Do you have any idea how they hurt me?" A vise tightened around Jilly's throat. Her eyes burned. She sank into the chair and tried to focus on the invoices spread out before her. "Don't even presume to barge in here and tell me how to run my life."

She held her breath waiting for Cam's retort. When only

silence answered, she cut her eyes toward him moments before the door slammed shut in his wake.

Sick and angry, she rolled the chair away from the desk and slumped forward. *I shouldn't have come here, God. No one understands. Especially not You. If You cared at all, You never would have let things end this way.*

She straightened with a groan and brushed the wetness from her cheeks. How many times had she told herself to stop dwelling on might-have-beens? Nothing could change the past.

Her gaze drifted around the pine-paneled room, sliding past photographs of Dogwood Blossom Inn's more prestigious guests—Harvey shaking hands with a famous Missouri-born actor, Alice accepting a kiss on the cheek from the St. Louis Cardinals manager, a group of state representatives and their spouses picnicking by the lake.

Then, next to the door, the embroidered sampler Alice had hung there years before, a verse from Psalm 68: A FATHER TO THE FATHERLESS, A DEFENDER OF WIDOWS, IS GOD IN HIS HOLY DWELLING. GOD SETS THE LONELY IN FAMILIES, HE LEADS FORTH THE PRISONERS WITH SINGING.

Once, long ago, Jilly had believed those words. No longer.

Her cell phone vibrated in the pocket of her khaki bermudas. Grateful for the distraction, she tugged out the phone, then suffered a moment of panic before reading the caller ID. Silverheels. Good. The harassing calls had all registered anonymous. "Hello?"

"Jilly, it's Therese. Thought you'd like to know your girls did really well in the tournament."

"Super. I tried to call Paul a few times over the weekend, but his voice mail kept picking up."

Therese's long exhalation whispered in Jilly's ear. "That's the other thing I wanted to let you know. Paul's been suspended."

The news slammed Jilly against the back of the chair. "What? Why?"

"Accusations were made by a couple of his students."

"Accusations?" Jilly raked her fingers through her hair. She thought again about the strange encounter in the men's room. Her stomach curled around itself.

"Let me just ask you, friend to friend." Therese's tone became secretive. "Have you ever seen Paul physically abusive with any of his students?"

"Abusive? As in, hit them?"

"Mm-hmm."

"Never. I've known Paul for years, and that's not like him at all." Even the men's room incident hadn't raised any suspicions about violence. The guys just seemed. . .intense.

"Okay, forget I said anything. Anyway, how much longer do you expect to be out of commission?"

Jilly stared down at her foot. "I've got this cast on for at least another month. I'll probably need a few weeks of physical therapy before I can compete again, but by midsummer I should be able to coach."

"Good. We need you."

"I promise, I'll be back in Modesto as soon as I possibly can."

❧

"How long do you think we can keep Jillian here?"

Cam cast Harvey a doubtful frown. "Probably not any longer than it takes for her ankle to heal. She still has a tennis coaching job waiting for her back in Modesto."

Harvey stared at the closed door to Alice's hospital room, worry deepening the furrows across his forehead. The doctor's latest report had not been encouraging. "I wish Jillian would come and see us. Alice won't stop asking about her. I know it would help if she could see her again."

Cam's jaw clenched. He'd tried again this morning to talk Jilly into coming to the hospital with him, but she'd refused. That girl could create more busywork than a stressed-out college professor. And Cam should know.

He thumped a knotted fist against his thigh. "Sometimes I could strangle that girl. How can she be so calloused?"

"Don't be so hard on her, Cam." Harvey trudged to a bench on the opposite wall and sank down.

"Don't be so hard on her? After how she's treated you and Alice?"

"She came out to help, didn't she? She didn't have to."

"And wouldn't have, if not for her broken ankle and being temporarily unemployed." Cam plopped onto the bench next to Harvey. "You're too forgiving. She doesn't deserve it."

Harvey shifted to stare at Cam, his face contorted. "Cameron Lane. I can't believe that came out of your mouth. You know better."

Remorse stabbed Cam's gut. He lowered his head. "I do know better. But it kills me to see you and Alice hurt like this."

"I'm pretty sure you wouldn't be judging Jillian so harshly if you weren't still hurting, yourself." Harvey patted Cam's arm. "Son, you've got to let go of the guilt. What happened to Terrance was not your fault."

"My head knows you're right." Cam huffed out a pained breath. "My heart doesn't agree."

"Then do whatever it takes to convince it otherwise."

A nurse exited Alice's room, and Harvey rose. "Any change? Can I see her now?"

She gave him a weary smile. "She's resting comfortably. Go on in. The doctor should be making rounds in another hour or so. He'll be able to tell you more."

Cam looked in on Alice for a moment before excusing himself to take care of some errands. He needed to pick up a few things from home and make sure the neighbor hadn't forgotten to feed Bart, Cam's gray tabby. Not that missing a meal or two would hurt the obese feline, but by now the litter pan contents could probably be classified hazardous waste.

On the drive across town, Cam couldn't get Alice's pale, haggard face out of his mind. Her atrial fibrillation was under control, but now she'd developed an infection. Cam didn't know what Harvey would do if he lost his beloved wife.

Again Cam wondered whether he should cancel the rest of his prayer retreats. He'd said as much to Harvey this morning, but the man wouldn't hear of it. Said Alice would rest better knowing business at the inn went on as usual.

Which of course sent Cam's thoughts careening back to Jilly Gardner. No more arguments, no more excuses. She would come into town to see Harvey and Alice this afternoon if Cam had to hog-tie her to the roof rack of his SUV.

❧

Jilly balanced on her crutches in the middle of the lobby, Cam on her left, Ralph on her right. Talk about double-teaming. Perspiration slid down her temples, as much from the stress of being cornered as from the modified weight training routine she'd just completed in the exercise room. "Okay, okay, I'll go see them. Give me time to shower and change."

She swiveled toward the family quarters and clunked to her room. The guys were right. She'd have to face Harvey and Alice eventually. Might as well get it over with.

Her left foot ensconced in a waterproof cast protector, Jilly clambered over the side of the claw-foot bathtub. She drew the curtain closed and eased onto the plastic patio chair Ralph had scrounged from among the inn's cast-off deck furnishings. With the shower spray pounding her shoulders, she pondered the latest reports about Alice's condition.

"Oh, God, please don't let her die."

The sudden surge of emotion stole Jilly's breath. She couldn't help herself—she loved the Nelsons, loved them dearly. And that was the root of her problem. They were supposed to be her forever family. They had promised. Talked to lawyers about adopting her. Gotten her hopes up. For three wonderful years she waited, prayed, grew to love Harvey and Alice as the father and mother she'd always longed for.

And then nothing. Three months after her seventeenth birthday, they told her it couldn't be worked out. No explanation, just apology after tearful apology. She'd given up trying to understand. Easier to focus on surviving her senior year and then leave the Nelsons—and the memories—behind when she headed off to college.

Salty wetness flowed down Jilly's face along with the shower stream. She turned off the water and flung back the curtain. Snagging a towel off the rack, she buried her face in its fresh-air softness. Alice always kept the family linens separate from the inn's. An old-fashioned clothesline and clean Ozark air imparted a fragrance no commercial laundry could duplicate.

A fragrance Jilly had come to associate with family and love.

She tossed the towel over the edge of the tub and hobbled out to her closet. Not much to choose from. She opted for an old pair of jeans she'd split partway up the left leg so her cast would fit through. A pink plaid shirt over a fuchsia tank top completed her attempt at casual chic. Wouldn't want the Nelsons to get the idea she'd dressed up for this visit.

Back in the lobby, it appeared Cam had won the coin toss for who'd be driving Jilly to town. She could have driven herself, and said as much, but both Cam and Ralph made it clear they didn't trust her to actually make it to the hospital.

At Blossom Hills General, Cam parked under the covered drop-off area and helped Jilly out of the Mariner. "I'll park and meet you inside."

She quirked her lips and glared. "I can find my own way to Alice's room. You don't have to babysit me."

"I should hope not." Cam slammed the driver's-side door and drove away.

A tremor snaked up Jilly's spine. With one look, Cam could make her feel twelve years old again and starving for his approval. Well, she didn't need it. His or anyone else's.

So why had she let him coerce her into this hospital visit?

"Because it's the right thing to do."

"Right for whom, God? You, me, or the Nelsons?" She tipped her head and stared at the underside of the roof. Her gaze settled on a moth caught in a spider's web. Exactly how she felt.

The electronic doors whispered open, and she limped inside. The atrium-like reception area glimmered under a ceiling of skylights. Ficus plants with braided trunks shed their dead leaves in massive clay planters. Bromeliads with spiky pink and orange flowers added a touch of color.

Jilly's one athletic shoe contributed its annoying squeak to the sound of her crutches tap-tapping across the marble floor. At the reception desk she waited for the white-haired volunteer to acknowledge her. "Can you direct me to Alice Nelson's room, please?"

The woman beamed a surprised smile and rose. Her abrupt motion sent the rolling office chair careening toward the lateral file behind her. "Oh my gracious. You're Jillian!"

Jilly gulped. "Yes."

"Well, aren't you a sight for sore eyes!" The elderly woman, whose nametag read MARGIE ALBERT, reached across the counter and clutched Jilly's hand. "It's been so long you probably don't recognize me. I'm Alice's cousin."

"Margie. How are you?" And how many more blasts from the painful past would Jilly have to endure? She glanced at the gnarled, age-spotted hands gripping hers and recalled the feisty, formerly raven-haired woman who used to toss tennis balls to her out behind the garage so she could practice her backhand. Dear Margie, yet another member of the family Jilly should have had.

"Why, I'm just fine, sweetie. Oh, it's so good to see you again!"

"You, too, Margie." She forced a smile. "Alice's room number?"

Margie gave her directions, and Jilly made her way to the bank of elevators, hoping she could get upstairs before Cam made it inside from the parking lot. The smaller her audience for this dreaded reunion, the better.

seven

At the sight of the tired-looking man with steel-gray hair, Jilly's heart stuttered. Harvey stood at the nurses' station, deep in conversation with a tall man in green scrubs. She edged toward them, wishing her crutches didn't creak so much.

Harvey stopped in midsentence and glanced over his shoulder. "Jillian."

"Hi, Harvey."

The fatigue drained from his face, and he seemed to grow three inches right before her eyes. He covered the distance between them in three long strides, reached out to hug her, then stopped short and cradled her face in his hands. Wetness pooled in the hollows alongside his nose. "Aw, sweetie, it's good to see you. You're as pretty as ever."

Jilly wobbled, her arms aching and tired after her weight workout earlier. "Mind if we sit down somewhere? I've been on my feet for a while—make that *foot*—and these crutches are killing me."

"There's a bench outside Alice's room. We can talk for a bit before you go in to see her." One hand hovering near her elbow, Harvey showed her the way.

"Cam told me the latest about Alice. I'm so sorry." Jilly lowered herself to the bench while Harvey propped her crutches against the wall.

"The docs are doing all they can." Harvey sighed and sat next to her. He reached for her hand, laced his fingers through hers, and squeezed. "I can't thank you enough for coming."

His palm felt cool and dry. His slim gold wedding band pressed between her knuckles. Beyond the nurses' station she saw Cam step off the elevator. Catching her eye, he gave a slight nod, then turned in another direction.

She fought the urge to leap from the bench, run him down, and insist he drive her straight back to the inn. As if she could run anywhere. The blue cast at the end of her left leg mocked her. Her lungs deflated on a barely muted groan.

Over the panicked hum filling her ears she heard Harvey speaking. "...so they're going to try a different antibiotic, and if she responds, we'll probably move her to a rehab hospital for a few weeks since the inn is so far from town."

"I see." She extricated her hand from Harvey's on the pretext of scratching her nose, then curled her fingers around the front edge of the bench. She touched something sticky—gum?—and scrubbed her fingertips on the leg of her jeans. "Will you stay in town with Alice until she's able to come home?"

"For the time being anyway. Church friends said I could use their guest room, but I'm staying here as much as I can." Harvey rubbed his chin. "You'll probably need to get back to Modesto before Alice is back on her feet, but if you'd show Ralph how to manage the front desk, he could help me keep things running."

"Speaking of which. . ." Jilly retrieved her crutches and pushed herself to a standing position. "I have some office work to finish up, and Heather and I still need to go over next weekend's menu."

"I won't keep you, then. Let's just look in on Alice for a minute." Harvey crossed the corridor and eased open the door. Glancing over his shoulder, he nodded at Jilly. "She's awake."

The hospital smells intensified inside the small private room. The lyrics of a soothing hymn flowed from a CD player. Several floral arrangements clustered on the wide windowsill, their subtle fragrance tickling Jilly's nose. She maneuvered into a position at the foot of the bed and let her gaze travel the length of Alice's frail body. Rheumy eyes stared back at her from beneath drooping lids. Silver-gray curls formed a halo around the pallid face.

Alice's mouth twitched into a semblance of a smile, and she wiggled the fingers of one hand. "Jillian."

Jilly bit down hard to keep her chin from quivering. She sniffed and drew the back of her hand beneath her nose. "Sorry. Allergies."

Harvey yanked a tissue from the box on Alice's nightstand and passed it to Jilly. "Forgot how bad your hay fever used to be."

"My allergies are even worse in Modesto." Jilly choked out a laugh. "Can't get away from them, I guess." *Can't get away from Alice and Harvey either.*

She drew a noisy breath. "Alice, I just wanted to come by and see how you're doing. Harvey says they're taking real good care of you."

Alice nodded and flicked her gaze toward the side of the bed, a clear signal she wanted Jilly to sit next to her.

Please, Cam, come and rescue me. Now!

When no knight in tarnished armor came to her aid, she gave a shrug and worked her way around to Alice's side. Handing off her crutches to Harvey, she perched next to Alice's hip. A huge knot tightened around her windpipe as Alice's hand crept into hers. Old feelings, old longings pulsed with every beat of her heart.

Slowly, slowly, Alice's eyes fell shut. Her chest rose and fell with peaceful regularity. Yet her hand stayed locked around Jilly's.

"She'll sleep for a while now." Freeing Jilly's hand, Harvey eased Alice's arm under the covers. "I knew your visit would help."

"I should get back to the inn." The words came with difficulty, as if someone had stolen her voice away. Jilly retrieved her crutches from Harvey and worked her way to the door.

If she stayed a moment longer, she'd shatter into a million pieces.

Harvey held the door for her, love and gratitude lighting his tired eyes. "You come back soon, okay? And if you need anything at all—"

"I know." She gave a crisp nod. "Good-bye, Harvey."

She found Cam on the bench outside the room. He looked up from a tattered *Newsweek* magazine and cast her a questioning smile. "Ready to go?"

❧

Cam had no idea a woman on crutches could move so fast. One moment Jilly was standing outside Alice's closed door, the next she'd plowed into Cam's chest.

And clearly not by accident.

The crutches fell away and would have crashed to the floor if Cam's reflexes had been any slower. While he snagged one with each hand, Jilly's arms wound around his neck, her face buried in his shoulder as her body shook with sobs.

"Hey, hey." He spoke gently while maneuvering both crutches to his left hand. He felt for the wall behind him and propped the crutches aside, then moved his hands up and down Jilly's back in a soothing rhythm. "Why the tears? Is Alice worse?"

"No, it's just—" A wet sniffle sounded in his ear. "Just get me out of here. Please."

"Okay, sure." He slid his index finger under her chin and raised her head until they made eye contact. With his thumb he smoothed away the wetness from one cheek. "Can you wait one minute? I'll say good-bye to Harvey and we'll be on our way."

Jilly nodded, and Cam swiveled her in a half-turn until he could ease her onto the bench. With a quick glance over his shoulder, he slipped into Alice's room.

Harvey rose from the recliner by the window. "Is Jillian all right?"

"She's a little shook up. I'm taking her back to the inn."
He wanted to ask what happened during Jilly's brief visit.
He wanted to ask what happened ten years ago that still
caused them all so much grief.

"You take good care of her, you hear?" Harvey wrapped his
fingers around Cam's forearm and squeezed, then returned to
the chair and reached for his Bible on the windowsill.

Cam cast a final glance at the sleeping Alice and edged
out the door. Wordlessly he helped Jilly to her feet and took
her downstairs. By the time he brought the car around, she
seemed more in control but not ready to talk. They drove
several miles in silence.

And in the silence Cam prayed. *Lord, there's obviously more
to this situation than either Jilly or the Nelsons have shared with
me so far. Show me how I can help.*

On the outskirts of Blossom Hills, Cam turned onto the
winding road leading to the inn. The forest closed in around
them, filtering the midday sun. Cam stole subtle glances at
Jilly, but in the shadowy interior of the SUV, her features
blurred. He had to pay attention to his driving anyway. The
twists and curves mimicked his jumbled thoughts.

He couldn't deny his loyalty and respect for the Nelsons.
Nor could he resist Jilly's tug on his emotions. He might not
want to admit it, but as a kid she'd wormed her way deep into
his heart, eliciting big-brother feelings that made him want
to protect and look out for her.

Only in the brother department, he'd already proven himself useless.

And the feelings he had for her now were anything but
brotherly.

He slammed his fist against the steering wheel. Jilly
jumped, and he shot her an apologetic frown. "Sorry. Just
thinking."

"Me, too." She blew out a gale-force sigh.

Up ahead, a painted wooden sign indicated the turnoff

to Dogwood Blossom Inn. Cam swung the Mariner up the narrow lane and pulled into the staff parking area behind the building. As he helped Jilly from the car, his gaze drifted toward the lake and the upturned fishing boat.

He gave Jilly's sleeve a tug. "You up for a boat ride?"

"I have office work to do." She looked down at her leg with a sad-eyed smirk. "Besides, I'm not exactly seaworthy."

"I doubt your cast will sink us. Give me a head start and by the time you limp down to the dock, I'll have the boat in the water." He winked. "Come on, it'll be fun."

Her quirked brow implied her doubts, but she nodded. "Why not? It's too nice a day to spend behind a desk."

Cam ducked into the storage shed to look for a couple of life vests, all the while wondering what had prompted this sudden idea. Something told him he needed to get Jilly to open up, finally talk about whatever had caused the rift between her and the Nelsons. Maybe if he could help her face her problems, it would begin to make up for how badly he'd failed Terrance.

&

A boat ride. Honestly.

Jilly made her way toward the lake with slow, mincing steps. No sense breaking her other ankle with a misstep on the uneven ground. She skirted the fire pit and didn't notice the crescendo of her thudding heart until she reached the gnarled old dogwood tree.

Oh, no. Were they still there, the initials she'd carved in the trunk all those years ago, the day after the *Braveheart* movie? She hoped Cam had never found them. JG + CL. How corny could a girl get?

"You coming or not?" Cam stood on the dock, one hand gripping a rope tied to the prow of the little green boat.

"Cool it, will you? I'm at a slight disadvantage, in case you hadn't noticed."

By the time she reached the dock, her ribs ached from the

pressure of the crutches, and she gladly handed them off to Cam. He took her by the elbow and helped her balance while he eased her arms into a life vest. Somehow he finagled her into the boat without tipping them into the drink.

Plying the oars, Cam aimed the prow toward an open area of the lake. A light breeze rippled the surface. It was one of those delicious late-spring days in the Ozarks that could be both chilly and warm at the same time. Jilly couldn't help smiling up at the vivid blue sky, puffy cotton-ball clouds playing hide-and-seek with the sun. The air tasted fresh and moist.

A couple hundred yards from shore, Cam stowed the oars. He blotted the perspiration from his forehead with his shirt-sleeve and heaved an appreciative sigh as his gaze traveled the tree-lined horizon. "Nothing like nature to put everything else in perspective. God's amazing, isn't He?"

"It's gorgeous out here, I have to agree." A tremor caught in Jilly's throat. The emotions she'd been suppressing since leaving the hospital came surging back.

"Want to talk about it?" Cam's voice grew quietly persuasive.

"I'm not sure I can."

Cam reached across the space between them and laid her fingers in his palm. "Come on, Jilly. Isn't it about time you dealt with whatever came between you and the Nelsons? Is ten years of resentment doing you or them any good?"

She released a shuddering sigh. "Obviously not."

Clutching both her hands, he gave them a small shake. "Then get it out. Tell me what was bad enough to keep you and the Nelsons apart all these years."

Jilly closed her eyes and dropped her chin to her chest. Every breath felt like an effort. "It's stupid. *I'm* stupid. It's my own fault. I should never have gotten my hopes up."

"About what?"

She met his confused gaze. A sigh raked her lungs. "About being adopted. They promised me. Harvey and Alice were supposed to be my"—Jilly's voice faltered; she could hardly speak the childlike term—"my forever family."

Cam straightened and shook his head. "They were going to adopt you? What happened?"

"That's just it. I don't know." Jilly yanked her hands free of Cam's and twisted on the seat. Her cast banged one of the oars. She grabbed her shin with one hand and the side of the rocking boat with the other. The *splat-splat* of the water against the hull kept time with her anxious breaths. Life vest or not, she could see her cast dragging her to the lake bottom like a cement block.

"Steady, it'll settle down in a minute." Cam slid to the other side of his seat, counterbalancing her weight shift. He gave a soft chuckle. "Didn't think to ask if you were afraid of water."

"Not afraid." Jilly swallowed the last remnants of panic. "Just not feeling very competent on land or sea these days."

"Understandable. How about I take us back to shore?"

"Good idea."

Cam reached for the oars. "So tell me more about this adoption thing. I never realized they'd even applied."

"They said it would be better to keep it between us until it was official." Jilly fixed her eyes on the dock as the memories sifted through her mind. "Guess they already had their doubts and didn't want a lot of explaining to do if it fell through." She grimaced. "Make that *when* it fell through."

"But you never found out what happened?"

"Figured they decided a teenage daughter was too much trouble after all."

❧

Cam reached for the whistling kettle and poured hot water over the spiced-apple teabags in two ceramic mugs. "Sugar?"

Jilly flicked her hair behind her ear. "Not the real stuff. One of those yellow sweetener packets, please."

He brought the mugs to the table and settled into the chair

next to hers. They sipped their tea in silence for several minutes, the warm kitchen and the hot drinks melting away the tightness in Cam's rowing muscles. He pondered Jilly's revelation—the Nelsons had planned to adopt her? He knew full well how much they loved her, how much they'd sacrificed so she could pursue her tennis dreams throughout junior high and high school. If the adoption fell through, it must have been as heartbreaking for Harvey and Alice as it was for Jilly.

Pushing his mug aside, Cam leaned forward and reached for Jilly's hand. "I'm sorry you had to go through such disappointment, but there has to be a valid explanation. Harvey and Alice wouldn't have given up so easily."

Jilly shrugged, her face a mask of cynicism. "If there is an explanation, they certainly never shared it with me."

"Did you ask?"

"Of course I did. I pleaded with them to tell me why. All they'd say was that they only wanted what was best for me. By the time I finished high school, it was like they couldn't ship me off to college fast enough."

"So you left Blossom Hills and never looked back."

Her voice quavered. "If they didn't care enough to fight for me, I didn't see any reason to stick around."

Cam stroked her hand and found himself wondering at its softness and yet its power. The calluses at the base of each finger. The hard places at the tips. These hands belonged to a woman of strength, determination, drive. Jilly knew how to go after what she wanted. Why, then—adoption or not—would she give up on the one part of her life that should mean the most, the love of two people who cared for her so deeply?

He met her teary gaze. "It's not too late, you know."

"Oh, please." She yanked her hand from his. "I made it this far without parents. I sure don't need them now."

Cam sat back and crossed his arms over his chest. "Why am I not convinced?"

She shot him a bemused stare, opened her mouth as if to speak, then snapped it shut. She drained the rest of her tea and fumbled for her crutches. "Think whatever you want. I have work to do."

Watching her hobble from the room, Cam fought the urge to go after her. He threaded his fingers through the handle of his mug and pressed it hard into his palm. If he couldn't undo his own mistakes, maybe he could at least do something to bring closure to Jilly and the Nelsons.

eight

Seated at Harvey's office computer, Jilly keyed in another prayer retreat registration and hit the ENTER key. This weekend Cam's participants were high-school students, which meant rooming girls with girls and boys with boys. Several of the seventeen registrants had specified a roommate. At least five had not. Now, was Lindsay Gibson a boy or a girl? And what about Devin Daley? Wouldn't do to accidentally mix genders. And Cam had said to assign the odd man out to share his room. What if the odd "man" turned out to be female?

"Aaack." Jilly shoved away from the desk and massaged her temples. She needed caffeine. Now.

"That bad, huh?" Heather sidled into the office and propped her hip on the corner of the desk.

"How do you feel about being overrun by teenagers?"

"Yeah, I heard." Heather's mouth drooped. "Figured they wouldn't appreciate tahini-glazed eggplant or gnocchi with truffle cream."

"Appreciate? I can't even spell that stuff!"

"Which is why we stocked up on pizza and burgers for the weekend." Heather pressed the back of her hand to her forehead. "Alas, my culinary talents will be wasted upon this horde of heathens."

Jilly checked her empty mug to see if she'd left even a drop of coffee in the bottom. No such luck. "Whip me up another cup of that orange mocha cappuccino you served at breakfast, and I'll appreciate you enough for a whole herd of teenagers."

"My pleasure." Heather slid off the desk. "Anything new about Alice?"

"Cam called from the hospital awhile ago. Said she's responding to the antibiotics." Stifling a rush of emotions, Jilly returned to the computer.

"That's encouraging. She's such a sweet lady. Back in a few with your 'ccino."

Heather's footsteps faded, and so did the words on the monitor. Jilly blinked away the blurriness and tried to concentrate on the next registration entry, but her mind kept spinning back to her conversation with Cam yesterday. He *had* to raise those haunting questions again, and just when she'd convinced herself she no longer cared.

Yeah, right.

Okay, so she did care. And always would, probably. But she didn't need Cam or anyone else constantly dredging up the past. Especially when her time at Dogwood Blossom Inn had already honed those feelings to razor sharpness.

And as if matters weren't difficult enough, now Jilly had to deal with the resurgence of her girlhood feelings for Cam. Why did she have to stumble straight from Alice's hospital room into his arms yesterday? Worse, why did he have to be so tender and sweet? Number one, he already had a serious relationship with that Liz person. Number two, even if he were available, Jilly would be returning to Modesto in a few weeks. It would be pointless to entertain anything more than friendship.

Pointless. She had to keep telling herself that.

❧

"This is pointless, Harvey." Cam wadded up his napkin and tossed it next to his empty pie plate. "Jilly has a right to know the truth about why you called off the adoption."

Harvey shifted sideways, his cafeteria chair creaking. "Playing tennis for Stanford was her dream. We couldn't take that away from her."

"I know, I know." Cam groaned at the irony of the whole situation. He'd finally extracted the full story from Harvey.

Jilly had just missed out on receiving one of Stanford's full athletic scholarships, but the school had offered her a partial instead. Even so, the Nelsons could never have afforded to cover the rest and were almost out of options when they learned of a supplemental scholarship available only to foster children. If they'd adopted Jilly, she would have become ineligible.

"It about killed us pretending there were other reasons the adoption didn't work out." Harvey rubbed his eyes. "You know how much Jillian wanted a real family. If we'd told her the truth, she'd have chosen us over Stanford, and then we'd have carried that guilt the rest of our lives."

"It's time to tell her, Harvey."

"What if she hates us even more?"

"She doesn't hate you." Cam clasped his hands on the table. "Anybody with a brain can see Jilly still loves you and Alice more than she can admit even to herself. It isn't too late for the three of you to be a family again. But it won't happen without honesty."

Harvey rubbed his eyes. "Guess you're right. Alice is doing a little better this afternoon. I could probably leave for a bit, drive out to the inn and talk to Jillian, if you think she'll listen."

"I'm betting she will." Cam gave a soft chuckle. "But you might score some extra points if you drop the 'Jillian' and just call her Jilly."

Laughter rumbled up through Harvey's chest. "Jilly, huh? Guess it does sound a bit sportier. I'll give it a try, but she'll always be my precious little Jillian."

Later, at his apartment, Cam sorted through some of the materials he planned to use for the youth prayer retreat. It was slow going, what with Bart padding across his lap and Cam's mind continually returning to his conversation with Harvey. *"Precious little Jillian"?* Cam snickered. What alternate universe had Harvey been living in? Jilly Gardner had always been a handful—stubborn, opinionated, determined—

He winced, and not from Bart's claws digging into his thigh. Nope, the truth hurt. The truth that those qualities were exactly what endeared Jilly to him. Exactly the reasons he found himself thinking about her more and more.

And less and less about Liz.

❧

Jilly had just sat down to supper with Heather and Ralph in the kitchen when the front door chime echoed over the intercom. "Who in the world could that be? Cam said he wouldn't be back until tomorrow morning."

Ralph rose. "You stay put. I'll go see."

"Don't be long," Heather called after him. "Lamb tagine tastes better when it's hot."

"These flavors are interesting, Heather. Tastes kind of—" Jilly's last bite of lamb lodged in her throat. At the sight of Harvey standing in the doorway, a sudden surge of panic stole her breath. "Oh no—is it Alice?"

"No, no, Alice is doing much better. Didn't mean to alarm you." Harvey ambled into the room and tucked his thumbs into his front pants pockets. "Thought maybe we could visit for a bit if you wouldn't mind."

Heather jumped up. "Have you eaten? I'll set another place."

"Smells mighty good." Harvey pulled out the empty chair across from Jilly. "Looks like you've outdone yourself again, Heather."

While Ralph and Heather took their seats, Jilly gave her anxious feelings a moment to subside. If Alice's condition had improved, then Jilly would soon be able to return to Modesto and get her life back on track. Surprisingly, the thought didn't give her the rush of anticipation she'd expected.

She tried to join in the dinnertime conversation but the edgy tone in Harvey's voice distracted her. He seemed nervous about something, pushing his food around his plate despite frequent compliments to the chef.

"You two aren't eating much." Heather rose to clear the serving dishes. "No baklava for you if you don't clean your plates."

Baklava. Jilly's lips creased at the mere thought of all that syrupy sweetness. "Save mine for later. Maybe I'll have it for a bedtime snack with a cup of that fantastic decaf Kona we had last night."

"You have Kona?" The anxiety briefly vanished from Harvey's eyes. "I'd love a cup."

"Great." Heather reached for the coffee carafe. "I'll start it brewing right now."

Ralph crumpled his napkin beside his empty plate. "Harvey, you got time to look at what I've done in the planter boxes out back?"

"Maybe later, Ralph. I need to talk about some stuff with Jillian." Harvey slid his gaze toward her. "I mean Jilly."

A strange letdown smothered Jilly's heart, for no reason she could explain except for Harvey's unexpected use of the nickname she'd been going by since her freshman year in college. Jilly was her grown-up name, her tennis persona. Suddenly—at least in Harvey's eyes—she only wanted to be Jillian.

Heather scooped coffee beans into the grinder. "If you two want to visit out on the deck, I'll bring the coffee as soon as it's ready."

"Sounds good." Jilly pushed up from the table and glanced around for her crutches. Ralph brought them over from where they'd been leaning against the pantry door. Irritated at her own helplessness, she closed her eyes for a second and breathed deeply. "Thanks."

Accepting help from others had always been hard for her, especially after she left the Nelsons behind and began the uphill struggle to make a name for herself in the tennis world. Yet even though she'd dedicated every spare moment and ounce of energy to the pursuit of tennis, her heart had gone out of it the day Harvey and Alice told her the adoption was off. From that time forward, she'd only been going through the motions. The trophies and accolades she'd hoped would fill her empty heart gradually meant less and less.

The sun had disappeared behind the hills by the time Jilly and Harvey settled into adirondack chairs on the deck. Stifling a shiver, Jilly forced a smile. "So what is it you needed to talk about?"

"Jillian—Jilly—" Harvey sat forward, his hand inches from hers. A sigh rasped between his tight lips. "It's time I explained why Alice and I called off the adoption."

"Called off the adoption." The words sliced upward through Jilly's chest. Harvey had never used that exact phrasing before. He and Alice had always talked around the subject with words like *"It just didn't work out,"* or *"You'll understand someday."*

Apparently, someday was today. Jilly stared into the half light and tried to follow the meandering trail of a lightning bug. "I'm listening."

"It was the scholarship. That and nothing more." With halting words, Harvey poured out the whole story of how they'd realized adoption would make her ineligible for the supplemental scholarship for foster children. "It was the hardest decision we ever had to make, but we couldn't take your dream away, even if it meant you'd hate us forever."

Jilly's breath froze in her lungs. She could hardly believe what she was hearing. Slowly, painfully, she shifted her gaze to meet Harvey's. His tortured expression surely matched her own.

"But don't ever, ever think we didn't want you," he went on, "didn't love you as our very own daughter. Don't love you still. Alice and I cherish you like—"

"Stop. Don't say it!" She couldn't bear to hear another word. *Take her dream away?* He just didn't get it, did he?

She sprang to her feet, crying out as her injured ankle

took her weight. She seized her crutches, fumbled to position them, dropped one. She nearly tripped over it as she lurched across the deck. The steps daunted her but only for a moment. She had to get away before she imploded.

She grabbed the handrail. Balancing on one foot, she lowered the lone crutch to the first step. She stepped off, teetered, then landed hard on her left foot. Pain ripped through her. As if watching a movie frame by frame she saw herself falling, falling, each wooden step pummeling another part of her body, until finally she lay sprawled on the grass, her world a white, pulsing scream of agony.

nine

At the sound of the doorbell, Cam tore his mind away from the Richard Foster book he'd been reading and checked the digital clock on his cable box. After seven. Who'd be dropping by this time of night?

"Move it, Bart. We've got company." He pushed the fat old cat off his lap and strode to the door.

"Hey, stranger." Liz stood on his front porch. "I come bearing pizza."

The aromas of cheese, pepperoni, and crispy garlic crust reminded him he hadn't eaten since lunch. On the other hand, Liz's untimely appearance stole away whatever appetite the pizza smells had conjured up.

"Wow. This is a surprise." What could he do but invite her in? He stepped aside and opened the door wider.

"I know I should have called first, but you'd have told me not to come."

Good guess. He noticed she was alone. "Where's Sammy?"

"Playing at a friend's. I don't have to pick him up until nine." She crossed in front of Cam and carried the pizza box and a weighty-looking plastic grocery bag into the breakfast nook. Her skintight jeans accentuated every curve. Her hips swayed with a deliberateness clearly meant to assault Cam's masculine sensibilities.

He drew up short and leaned against one side of the kitchen archway. "What are you doing, Liz?"

"Bringing you supper. What does it look like?" She cast him an innocent smile before going to the cupboard for plates and napkins. "Want to pour us some drinks? I brought diet cola for me and root beer for you. The caffeine-free kind." Another

71

smile, this time with a wink. "See, I remembered."

Frustration rolled through Cam's chest. He should be flattered, but all he felt was annoyance. He pulled a hand down his face and stepped closer. "Liz—"

"Want to eat at the table or on the sofa?" She snagged a metal turner from the utensil drawer and served them each two slices of pizza.

"Liz."

Her hand froze above the plate. "What is it, Cam? You look upset."

"I'm not upset. It's just. . ." How could he explain without hurting her? The feelings—if he'd ever really had any for her—were no longer there.

She faced him, her shoulders drooping. "I understand. Your mind's a million miles away on your retreat stuff or whatever. And I barged in without calling or even considering you might already have eaten or maybe weren't in the mood for pizza or—"

The kitchen extension shrilled. Grateful for the interruption, Cam shot Liz an apologetic frown and reached for the receiver.

"Cam, it's Harvey." His voice sounded strained, urgent. "Can you meet me at the hospital?"

Cam's heart plummeted. Alice must have taken another bad turn. "I can be there in twenty minutes. Are you there now?"

"No, I'm at the inn. The ambulance is about to leave with Jilly, and I'll be—"

"Wait. *Jilly?*" Harvey's words ping-ponged through Cam's skull. "What happened?"

"She took a bad spill off the deck. I'll tell you more when we get to the hospital."

"Okay then. Tell her—" The line went dead.

With numb fingers, Cam set the receiver on the base. He pressed his palms against the beveled edge of the counter and closed his eyes in prayer. *Father, please let Jilly be okay. Help her*

*know how much You love and care for her. How much Harvey
and Alice and I all—*

"Cam, honey?"

He jerked his head around. Liz stood right behind him. "I
have to go to the hospital."

"I gathered that. Something happened to Jilly?"

"A fall. That's all I know." With a shrug he turned to face
her. "Sorry about the pizza." *Sorry about everything.*

Liz tucked her hands against his sides. "Is it so important
for you to be there? I mean, really, what can you do?"

"I don't know. But I need to go." He took her wrists and
gently moved her aside, then grabbed his keys and wallet
from the end of the counter. "Can you let yourself out?"

"Let me go with you, honey. I can see how worried you
are." She snatched her purse off a kitchen chair.

The breath rushed from his lungs. The last thing he
wanted was Liz at the hospital with him. He choked out
a laugh and imbued his voice with forced lightness. "How
quickly we forget. Don't you remember when Sammy cut his
foot last spring? You had me take him to the ER because you
were afraid you'd pass out."

A sick look flickered across Liz's face. "Okay, so I have a
thing about blood. But will you call me? I could wait for you,
keep the pizza warm."

Halfway through the door to the garage, Cam spun around
and gripped Liz's shoulders. The confusion and disappointment clouding her expression made his heart ache. "Please go
home, Liz. I have no idea how long I'll be. And you'll need to
pick up Sammy soon anyway."

"But—"

"Please. I'll call you." He yanked the door closed behind
him and punched the garage door opener. As the heavy door
rumbled along its track, he climbed behind the wheel of his
SUV and said another prayer.

Father, whether there's a chance for something between Jilly and me or not, I know I'm about to hurt Liz, and there's nothing I can do about it. Help me handle this with as much grace and compassion as I can.

❧

Slowly, unwillingly, as if being dragged down a long, echoing corridor, Jilly felt awareness return. Every sound seemed amplified—garbled voices, wheels rolling across a hard floor, the clatter of metal against metal.

And a sound she didn't recognize. Breathing? No, more like snoring.

Light filtered between her fluttering eyelids. She squinted against the streaks of sunlight cutting through the half-closed vertical blinds and struggled to remember where she was. When she tried to lift her arm, the tug of an IV tube answered her question.

Great. I'm in the hospital.

Her stomach heaved. She swallowed down the nausea as her mind retraced the events that had brought her here. Supper with Harvey. His confession about the Stanford scholarship. The rage and disbelief that propelled her across the deck and sent her tumbling down the steps.

The rasping snores deepened. She forced her thoughts to the present. Easing her head to the left in search of the source, she glimpsed Cam sprawled in a recliner.

A new emotion warmed her chest. Her breath hitched. She blinked several times and reached up to brush away a sudden spurt of tears. How long had he been sitting there? And why?

He stirred, opened his eyes, straightened. Grinned. "Hey, kiddo, when did you wake up?"

"Just a minute ago." Her throat felt raspy. She tried to cough.

"Here, the nurse said you could have ice chips." Cam reached for an insulated plastic container and offered her a spoonful of shaved ice.

The coolness soothed her dry mouth. "How long have I been out?"

"Pretty much since your surgery last night."

"Surgery?" More nausea, this time accompanied by raw panic. She did a quick mental survey of her body parts. Everything felt intact, if stiff and sore. Then she noticed the dull ache in her left leg and the bulge under the blanket where her broken ankle was propped up. She raised questioning eyes to Cam.

He eased onto the side of the bed and took her hand. "Jilly, you reinjured your ankle. It was pretty torn up. They had to put it back together with pins and I don't know what all."

"Terrific." She looked away, her breath coming in short, sharp gasps.

"Your doctor will be able to explain it better—how serious the break was, what your recovery will entail."

Every exhalation scraped against her wounded heart. "I don't need a doctor to tell me my tennis career is over."

Cam pressed her hand against his chest. She could feel his heartbeat beneath his nubby pullover. "Jilly, I want you to know I'll be here for you. I mean, Harvey and I both—"

"Please, don't!" She yanked her hand away and rolled her torso toward the window. As much as she could anyway, with her left leg pretty much useless and the rest of her feeling like she'd been trampled by a herd of wild horses.

With gentle firmness Cam took her by the shoulders and made her look at him. "I know about the scholarship. I know that's why Harvey and Alice called off your adoption. And I know you're angry and confused. But you have to believe they did it because they love you. They loved you too much to keep you from your dream."

"My dream?" Bitterness seared her throat. "My dream was to have a real family. A real home. A mom and dad who would always be mine."

"Do you think an adoption certificate would have made

Harvey and Alice love you any more than they already do? They gave up their dream, too, in case you didn't notice. But that's what love is. Sacrificing your own happiness for someone else's."

"They gave up their dream, too." Jilly had never considered the Nelsons' disappointment might equal her own. An immense weight of shame and regret pressed down upon her. She'd wasted ten long years resenting the Nelsons for a decision they made out of the purest love.

"If they'd only told me why, if they'd only given me the choice. . ." Tears cascaded down her face. She couldn't bring herself to look at Cam. "I need to be alone now. I just need to be alone."

≈

Seated on a hard plastic chair in Alice's room, Cam stifled a yawn. He pressed his hands against his thighs. "I should get out to the inn soon. Those teenagers will start arriving in a few hours, and with Jilly out of commission, I told Ralph I'd help him at the front desk."

"After spending all night at the hospital?" Harvey tucked Alice's covers around her and tugged her pillow higher. "You're dead on your feet, son. Maybe you should cancel the retreat."

"We'll manage." Cam rose, exhaustion dragging on every muscle. "If I leave pretty quick, I can grab a nap before the kids start showing up."

Alice slapped away Harvey's fussing fingers and motioned Cam over. "Are you sure Jillian's going to be all right? Do you think she'll forgive us?"

"Give her some time to let it all sink in." He glanced at Harvey and saw the guilt and worry carved into his face. "Don't blame yourself for Jilly's fall. She needed to know the truth, no matter how much it hurt."

Harvey sighed and paced to the window. "Yeah, I know. And I know it's no good wondering if we should have handled things differently ten years ago. Got no choice now but to keep trusting the Lord to heal Jillian's heart and her body."

"He will. . .in time." Cam smiled down at Alice and smoothed one of her silver curls away from her face. "Just like He's healing you. Sure glad to know you're doing better."

"Oh, I'm coming along fine." She aimed a scowl at Harvey. "Which is why I'm sending this man back to the inn with you. He's nothing but a nuisance here, fussing around like an old tom turkey. Better he burns off his nervous energy helping you ride herd on those teens."

"Now, Alice," Harvey began.

"No argument. You two get on out of here so Cam has time to put his feet up for a bit." Alice aimed her index finger at Harvey's chest. "Wouldn't hurt you to sleep in a real bed for a change either, old man. One more night in that recliner and your body's going to petrify in a permanent S-shape."

Cam raised an eyebrow and started for the door. "Harvey, I think we'd better do as Alice says. She's looking almost fit enough to leap out of that bed and wallop us good if we don't."

He and Harvey shared a laugh on the way to the parking lot. It felt good to relieve some of the tension shrouding them both. At the inn, Cam went straight up to his room and stretched out on the bed without even turning back the quilt. He fell asleep in minutes.

❧

Jilly jerked awake. She'd been dozing off and on for two days, as if her body couldn't quite purge itself of the anesthesia. At least the nausea had subsided.

But the tears had not. When a nurse came in to check on her and saw the dampness on Jilly's pillow, she jammed a thermometer between Jilly's lips to make sure she wasn't running a fever. Noticing Jilly's tears, she handed her a tissue. "You had a really bad break, and it's scary, I know. Would you like to talk to someone? The chaplain, or maybe a psychologist?"

Talking was the last thing Jilly felt like doing. It was too soon. She gave her head a shake and willed away the grogginess. Finding the bed control, she pressed the button to raise her head. "Just tell me when I can get out of here."

The nurse checked Jilly's chart. "The doctor's still concerned about a possible concussion and those rib contusions. He wants you to stay one more night for observation. If everything looks good tomorrow, we'll get a new cast on that ankle and you can go home."

Home. Where was home anymore? Most likely she didn't have a tennis career to go back to. And even if the ankle strengthened enough to allow her to coach again, no way could she expect Therese to hold her job indefinitely.

The nurse opened the door to leave and suddenly halted. Turning to Jilly, she said, "You have a couple of visitors, honey." She stepped out of the way as Harvey pushed Alice's wheelchair into the room.

"Oh, my baby Jillian!" The smile on Alice's face stretched wide. Her eyes crinkled at the corners, and tears seeped out. She reached up to slap Harvey's hand. "Come on, you old coot. You can move faster than that. I need to hug my girl!"

Harvey rolled the wheelchair close enough that Alice could lean up and plant a kiss on Jilly's cheek. "She wouldn't wait a minute longer," Harvey said. "I've been looking in on you, but you seemed to need sleep more'n you needed company."

A tumble of emotions sent Jilly's heart thudding. The tears she'd been fighting for two days burst forth anew. "I'm sorry," she said. "I'm so, so sorry."

Harvey rushed around to the other side of the bed and carefully pulled her into his arms. "We're the ones who are sorry, darlin'. Can you ever forgive us?"

One arm tucked against Harvey's warm chest, her other hand snuggled into Alice's amazingly firm grip, Jilly felt the last remnants of resentment drain out of her. Oh, how she loved these people! How she needed them! All the words she longed to say jammed against one another and couldn't escape. A phrase from Alice's sampler filled her mind: *"God sets the lonely in families. . . ."*

She could only smile through the flood of tears and hope Harvey and Alice could read the love in her eyes. *Please, God, forgive me. Help me somehow make up for all the lost years we could have had together. The Nelsons are my family and always will be.*

ten

Cam stepped behind the lectern on the chapel dais to close the Sunday-morning worship segment of his teen retreat. "Let's take a few minutes now for personal prayer requests." He jotted notes as the group called out special concerns. When the room grew silent, he asked everyone to bow their heads. As he lifted up each concern, he drew on scripture to claim God's promise of healing, hope, strength, and salvation.

"Finally, Father," he said, hands clasped atop his notes, "heal and comfort my friend Jilly. Help her to know Your love. Show her that You can always be counted on, no matter what difficulties or disappointments she faces. In Christ's name, amen."

A murmur of amens whispered through the chapel, and Cam dismissed the group for lunch. By the time he gathered up his notes and Bible, the teens had moved into the dining room. Crossing the quiet lounge, he heard Ralph call his name and detoured to the lobby.

"Thought you'd want to greet our arrival." Ralph stood at the inn's double entry doors, one pulled wide as Harvey wheeled Jilly through. Her left leg rested on a wheelchair extension supporting her ankle cast.

Jilly grinned at him. "Sorry I left you in the lurch. You surviving all those wild and crazy teenagers?"

Cam couldn't explain the sudden elation swelling his chest. Where moments ago he'd been fighting a midday slump, renewed energy surged. He loped across the floor and halted at Jilly's side. He reached out and tousled her hair, and the feel of it under his fingers brought back memories of a thick brown ponytail. "You'll do anything to get out of work. Even throw yourself down a flight of steps."

Jilly gave a wry smile. "Not a technique I would recommend."

"Didn't think so." Cam shot a questioning glance at Harvey, whose eyes sparkled with happiness. Apparently Jilly and the Nelsons were working out their differences.

"Just in time for lunch," Ralph said. "Heather's whipped up some gourmet burgers and seasoned oven fries you have to taste to believe."

Fatigue lengthened Jilly's face. She cast Ralph a regretful look. "Maybe you could have her save me some?"

"Sure thing. You coming, Cam?"

Sounds of laughter and noisy conversation filtered from the dining room. Right now, it was the last place Cam wanted to be. "Would you tell the kids I'll be there in a few minutes? I'll help Harvey get Jilly settled."

Ralph shot him a knowing wink. "Take your time, bud."

As Harvey wheeled Jilly into the family quarters, Cam got the doors and made sure no obstacles barred their path. In Jilly's room, he helped Harvey lift her onto the bed. While Cam propped pillows behind her back and under her ankle, Harvey excused himself to get the rest of Jilly's things from the car. He returned with a small overnight bag and a walker.

Jilly took one look at the aluminum contraption and groaned. "As if crutches weren't bad enough, now I have to shuffle around like a little old lady."

Cam couldn't resist a chuckle. "Glad my digital camera has movie mode. That's gonna go over big on YouTube."

"Try it and I'll dig up those snaps I took of you with your mullet."

"Hey!" Cam gave her a playful slap on the arm. "I was a doofus teenager at the time."

Harvey stepped between them. "That's enough, you two, or I'll pull out a few incriminating photographs of my own." He bent to kiss Jilly's forehead. "I'll make sure things are running smoothly out front before I head back to town. You sure you're gonna be okay?"

Love shone in her eyes. She squeezed his hand. "I'll be fine, Harvey. And tell Alice to keep getting better so she can come home, too."

"I'll be back to check on you in a sec," Cam told her, following Harvey out. In the lobby he pulled Harvey aside. "Haven't seen you this happy in a long time. Jilly either, for that matter. Are things as good between you as they look?"

"We're getting there." Harvey nodded, his mouth curving in a satisfied smile. Then his expression turned grim. "I'm more worried about how she's going to handle giving up tennis. She's putting up a brave front, but it's gotta be breaking her heart."

Cam shook his head. "I keep praying there's still a chance she can play again."

"You'll keep a close eye on her this weekend?"

"You betcha."

While Harvey headed for the office, Cam made a quick trip to the kitchen, where he had Heather prepare a burger and fries for Jilly. He filled a glass with iced tea, then carried the tray to Jilly's room.

She looked up in surprise. "Aw, Cam, you didn't need to do that."

"My pleasure, m'lady." He waited while she laid a pillow across her lap, then set the tray on top of the pillow. "Missing anything?"

She checked the hamburger trimmings. "Looks perfect. You even remembered I don't like mayo."

"There's a lot I remember about you." Cam stuffed his hands into his back pockets, boyish shyness warming his face. At her curious glance, he went on, "Like, I remember you could never do your homework without the TV on in the background. And your favorite color is red. And you don't want an anchovy within ten miles of your pizza, but you like them in your caesar salad."

Jilly grinned. "Wow. Didn't know you were paying attention."

"You were a hard girl to ignore."

"Were?"

"Still are." He stared at the toes of his sneakers and hoped she couldn't detect the throb of his pulse beneath his jaw.

She cleared her throat. "Shouldn't you be getting back to your retreat kids?"

"Oh. Yeah, I guess so." He spotted her purse on the end of the bed and moved it within reach. "Is your cell phone on? I've got mine on vibrate. If you need anything at all, just give me a buzz. If I'm tied up, I'll send Ralph or Heather right away."

Jilly sighed and gave a meaningful eye roll. "Please. I've got my walker, lunch, and the TV remote. What more could a girl need?"

"Okay, if you're sure. . ." Cam edged toward the door. Halfway into the hall, he stopped. Turned. Shot her a squint-eyed stare. "You really have a picture of me with my mullet?"

❧

The moment Jilly heard the outer door close behind Cam, she set the lunch tray aside. Easing onto her right hip, she reached to open the nightstand drawer. It slid out with the familiar squeaks and moans from her childhood. With a practiced motion she lifted the entire drawer onto her lap and tipped it until she could run her searching fingers along the bottom.

Seconds later she secured her prey, a thin manila envelope taped to the underside of the drawer. She moved the drawer to the other side of the bed and emptied the envelope contents onto her lap, a giggle erupting as adolescent memories tumbled through her thoughts along with the color snapshots that now lay before her—every single one of them a picture of Cam.

She found the one she'd been looking for—Cameron Lane, age sixteen, thin and lanky and solemn-faced. He wore Levi's

501 jeans and a brown T-shirt bearing a sketch of Jesus with outstretched arms and the words SEE HIS NAIL-SCARRED HANDS.

"Ah, yes, the year of the mullet." Jilly shook her head and laughed at the image of Cam with super-short hair all over his head except for the long fringe around the nape. Blackmail material indeed.

Except back then Jilly had thought him the handsomest, coolest guy on the face of the planet.

Her stomach did a roller-coaster loop-the-loop. The mullet was history, but Cam Lane remained as handsome as ever. She shivered at the memory of his fingers ruffling her hair. Could he ever think of her as anything but the pesky kid she used to be?

Did she want him to?

She plopped her head against the pillow and released a long, slow sigh.

She did. She definitely did.

❧

On Monday morning, Jilly determined to get back to work. She sat sideways at the desk in Harvey's office, her left leg propped on a cushioned footstool. With Ralph's help, she'd rearranged the computer setup to make it easier to reach the keyboard from this awkward position.

She'd been hard at it for two hours now, and the entries in the financial software program blurred before her eyes. With a groan, she pushed the keyboard aside and pressed her palms into her eye sockets.

"You don't have to do this, you know."

At the sound of Cam's voice, her hands fell to her lap. She offered him a weak but grateful smile. "I felt useless lying around watching TV all weekend while everybody else looked after your teen group."

"We managed fine." Cam pulled over a chair and straddled it, resting his forearms on the back. "At least take a book out to the deck and enjoy some fresh air. It's too gorgeous a day to be cooped up in front of a computer screen."

The view of the sun-dappled deck and the lake beyond did look tempting. Jilly frowned, then shook her head. "Work is better for me right now."

As she reached for another invoice from the stack, Cam laid his hand on her arm. "Harvey said he'd be home later to help catch up. Come outside with me."

The warmth of his hand penetrated her thin T-shirt sleeve. She didn't know which was worse—facing the possible end of her tennis career or confronting her growing attraction to a man who was completely unavailable. "No boat rides, okay?"

"No boat rides." He stood and set her walker in front of her, steadying it as she pulled herself upright.

"So what are you still doing here?" she asked on the way through the lobby. "Don't you have a life beyond the prayer retreats?"

He chuckled and held the door for her. "Me, a life? You've got to be kidding!"

Something in his voice tugged at her senses. She eased into one of the adirondack chairs and allowed Cam to lift her cast onto the matching wooden ottoman. Choosing her words with care, she asked, "Don't you miss that little boy? And his mom?"

A pained look settled around Cam's eyes. He sighed through his nose. "Can we talk about something else?"

"Okay." She'd hit a nerve, obviously. She'd suspected all along his feelings for the woman and her son were stronger than he wanted to admit. A heavy emptiness pressed down on her. Guess she really was still just a kid in Cam's eyes. The extra attention he'd been lavishing on her all weekend had been that of a concerned big brother, nothing more.

"Sorry, Jilly, didn't mean to snap at you." Cam sank onto the edge of the ottoman, facing at a slight angle from her. He locked his clenched hands between his knees. "It's just. . .Liz and I need to have a serious talk soon. She's pushing for more than I'm ready for."

Jilly's heart did a slow roll. This emotional seesaw ride just never seemed to end. "I see." *Not.*

He squared his shoulders and met her gaze. "Enough about me. What's going on with you? And don't pretend everything's okay. You've had more trauma in one weekend than most people face in a lifetime."

She shrugged, the breath rushing out of her lungs. "I'm a washed-up, out-of-work tennis pro with no clue what happens next. What do you want me to say?"

"I want you to say how it makes you feel. Yell. Scream. Cry. Whatever it takes."

In spite of the ache in her soul, she wanted to laugh. "You're a guy. Guys don't usually want to deal with feelings, much less the screaming and crying."

"Yeah, well, I thought you might appreciate seeing my sensitive side." He took her hand, and all rational thought flew from her mind.

What were we talking about?

Oh, yeah. Her emotional state. Just a wee bit haywire at the moment. Must be the new pain meds she'd been on since the surgery.

"Jilly?"

She widened her eyes in a vain attempt to clear both her vision and her brain. Cam, pain medication, and the sunshine warming her shoulders made for a dangerous combination. His hand still held hers, and it felt so nice. "Cam, really, you don't need to worry about me. I'll be okay."

"You always were too independent for your own good." Resignation darkened his eyes. "But just know I'm here for you if you ever feel like talking."

Talking? Cam's nearness pulled all moisture from her mouth. She swallowed. Her gaze slid to his lips. "I, uh. . .sure."

❧

Cam tossed his razor and toothbrush into his travel kit and zipped it shut. He should have hit the road hours ago, before Jilly's plucky resilience tunneled any deeper into his heart. That languid look in her eyes as they sat on the deck nearly undid him. But he didn't dare deal with his growing feelings for Jilly until he broke things off with Liz.

Lord, help me do it right.

He hadn't driven halfway back to town when his cell phone chirped. When he read Liz's name and number on the caller ID, his pulse ramped up. He took a steadying breath before answering and struggled for a nonchalant tone. "Hi, Liz. What's up?"

"Where are you, honey?" She sounded peeved.

"Just now heading home from the retreat."

"I knew you wouldn't want to be bothered during your prayer thing, but I've been worried." A pause. "You never called to let me know what happened at the hospital."

Cam's stomach clenched. "Guess I got busy and forgot." He saw a turnout up ahead and pulled over. No sense risking an accident. This conversation had already proved too distracting.

"Well? Is that all you have to say?" Her voice shook. "Do I mean so little to you that you can't spare two minutes to let me know what's going on?"

"I didn't mean to ignore you. I'm sorry." Cam released his seat belt buckle and rested his forehead on the steering wheel. Shame and regret curdled his insides. Whatever his feelings for Liz—or lack thereof—she deserved better than this.

And he called himself a Christian.

He hauled in another deep breath. "Where are you calling from? Can we meet somewhere?"

"I'm at Riley's. My shift ends at two-thirty. I'll have an hour before I have to pick up Sammy from school."

Cam mentally ran through Liz's route from the pharmacy to Sammy's school. Halfway between was the Something's Brewing Café. He checked his watch. Not quite two. Still time to drop his things at home and check on Bart. "What if I meet you at Something's Brewing around two forty-five?"

"I. . .guess that would be okay." The pout in her tone chafed his nerves.

All the more reason to bring this relationship to a timely end.

eleven

At least with the walker, Jilly didn't have the problem of sore ribs from the crutches, but even though she'd tried to keep up a modified workout routine, bearing weight with her arms grew tiring after a while. As she contemplated another trek from her room to the front desk, the wheelchair looked mighty tempting.

Nope, not ready to settle for invalid status. She gritted her teeth and reached for the walker.

Harvey met her in the hallway. He'd taken to sleeping in his own bed the past couple of nights, now that Alice had been moved to the rehab hospital. "Mornin', sleepyhead. On your way to breakfast?"

"Already ate. Just came back to brush my teeth." Jilly inched the walker forward and slid-hopped her right foot along behind it. She stopped long enough to press one finger under her nose before a sneeze erupted, then dug a tissue from the pocket of her shorts.

"You taking anything for those allergies?"

"My prescription meds usually help a lot, but I got distracted when I ordered my refill and forgot to give this address. I'm trying to stretch out my doses until my landlady forwards the package." She continued down the hall, and Harvey edged around her to open the door into the lobby.

"I'm heading into town to sit with Alice awhile," he said. "Want to come along?"

Jilly eyed the overflowing in-box on the front counter. "I'd love to, but it's Wednesday already. I should catch up on more paperwork before things get busy with Cam's next retreat."

"Aw, this looks like mostly junk mail." Harvey riffled through the stack and tossed several items into the recycle bin beneath the counter. "Besides, you've been working way too hard for somebody who's just had surgery."

"I'd rather work than sit around twiddling my thumbs." Jilly eased onto the barstool behind the counter and set her cast on the footrest. She didn't add that keeping busy kept her mind off other things. Like the end of her career. Like losing ten years with the two people who loved her most. Like falling for a guy who probably still thought of her as a selfish, spoiled kid.

After all, Cam hadn't so much as called since he left the inn Monday afternoon.

She sneezed and grabbed a tissue from the box next to the phone. "You go on, Harvey. Give Alice a big hug for me. I promise I'll visit her in a few days."

"All right, have it your way. But don't feel like you have to do it all. I'll be back this afternoon, and I'll be in and out all weekend, too."

When the back door closed behind Harvey, Jilly let the breath whoosh from her lungs. She'd tried, really tried to stay upbeat for his sake. He carried too much blame already for the lost years, and now for her fall and new injuries. She couldn't let him see the panic lurking just beneath the surface, the stark dread of an empty, meaningless future.

She knotted a fist and hammered the countertop. There *must* be some way to get back to tennis. If she found a topnotch orthopedist, worked hard at physical therapy—it *couldn't* be the end of the line for her. *Oh, please, God!*

❧

Beneath the greenery in the rehab hospital atrium a fountain burbled, its gentle sounds muting the conversations going on around Cam and Alice. He'd stopped by for a visit this morning, his first since she'd been moved. "Nice place. Are they treating you okay?"

"Never a dull moment. They'll have me fit for a marathon

in no time." Alice touched his shoulder. "You look down today, Cam. Something bothering you?"

His breath seeped out through tight lips. "I broke it off with Liz."

"Oh, honey, I'm sorry. Did something happen between you?"

"More a case of what *wasn't* happening." Cam shifted on the window seat next to Alice's tropical-print lounge and stretched one leg out. "I'm not sure I ever had feelings for her. If not for Sammy, we might never have gotten together in the first place."

Alice chuckled. "I remember when you first started tutoring that little boy as part of your church's afterschool program. You bragged on him like crazy."

"He's one great kid." Cam massaged the back of his neck. "But I can't base a relationship with Liz strictly on the fact that I've gotten attached to her son."

"That's true. It wouldn't be fair to either of them, or to you."

"I could probably continue tutoring Sam, but I'm not sure it's a good idea." He glanced at Alice, hoping she'd tell him otherwise.

She didn't, of course. "I know you'll miss him. And you'll both grieve for a while. But you'll both be fine, in time."

Footsteps echoed on the tile floor. Cam looked up to see Harvey striding their way. Lifting his hand in greeting, he scooted sideways so that Harvey could sit next to Alice.

"There's my beauty queen." Harvey dropped a kiss on Alice's cheek before joining Cam on the window seat. "The nurses told me you were off gallivanting with some handsome young man."

"Well, since there weren't any handsome *old* men to escort me, I didn't have much choice." Alice wedged her hand into Harvey's, and they shared a loving glance.

Cam's heart warmed. If only he could hope for a lasting relationship of his own someday.

"Our Cam's had a difficult few days," Alice said. "He and

Liz are no longer together."

Harvey swiveled to face Cam. "Is that true?"

Cam gave a halfhearted shrug. "We had a long talk Monday afternoon. I told her I couldn't see a future between us."

"How'd she take it?"

"Hard. Typical Liz." Cam lowered his head, fingers laced between his knees. The hateful words she'd spewed—most of them about Jilly—still burned his ears. "I always knew she had a jealous streak. It came out in spades when I told her it was over."

"Honestly, son, I can't say I'm sorry. Liz just never seemed your type." Harvey patted Cam's leg. "God has someone special in mind for you. For Liz, too, if she'd ever open her heart to receive Him."

"That was probably our biggest problem. She claimed to believe in God, but her life never evidenced any level of faith."

Alice made a *tsk-tsk* sound. "All you can do for a person like her is to keep praying. And I will."

Just one more reason Cam loved the Nelsons so much. A half smile quirked his lips. "Alice, with you praying for her, Liz's salvation is as good as secured."

"There's somebody else we should all be praying for." Harvey looked from Alice to Cam. "I'm worried about Jillian. And I'm not talking about her broken ankle."

❧

Jilly sprawled on the sofa in the Nelsons' cozy den, her cell phone pressed to her ear. "Hi, Therese, how's it going?"

"Jilly, I'm glad you called. How much longer before you can be back on the courts?"

Jilly clamped her teeth together. She couldn't make her circumstances sound too dire, or Therese would ask for her resignation on the spot. "I've had some complications with my ankle. It's going to take a little longer to heal than I expected."

"Oh, man." Therese drew out the words with a groan. "We

are really hurting here. Paul is nowhere to be found, the sub we hired can never seem to get to work on time, and with summer here we've got a two-page waiting list of new students."

It felt great to be needed, but Jilly couldn't see any way to resolve Therese's dilemma. At least not in the foreseeable future. She focused on the first part of her boss's statement. "What happened with Paul?"

"I told you we had to suspend him because of those accusations." Therese huffed. "Now the cops want to question him, but it looks like he's skipped town."

"The cops? Why?"

"We're keeping a tight lid on it because we don't want the club's rep to suffer." Therese lowered her voice. "Jilly, they're saying Paul's kids were doing steroids, and the cops want to know if he was involved."

Jilly choked on a breath. "Steroids! Last time we talked, you said Paul had been accused of physical abuse."

"That's what we all thought at first. Then the cops dug deeper and ended up questioning three or four of Paul's students. Those families have since cancelled their club memberships, and I heard the kids have been permanently banned from their high-school tennis teams." Therese's voice dropped another notch. "Did you ever see *anything* suspicious, either on or off the courts?"

A sick feeling churned in Jilly's gut. The men's room. Her fall from the stepladder. The threatening phone calls.

A knock sounded on the outer door. "Jilly, you there?" Ralph's voice.

"Hold on a second, Therese." Jilly's brain felt like mush. She didn't need one more thing. "It's open, Ralph."

He appeared in the den doorway. "Sorry to interrupt, but you've got a visitor from Modesto."

While Jilly scrambled to process this information, a blond head appeared over Ralph's shoulder.

Paul!

She looked from the former Silverheels tennis coach to the cell phone in her left hand. Everything Therese had just told her raced through her mind. Paul missing. . .the cops. . .steroids. Half of her wanted to snap the phone shut and immediately dial 911. The other half remembered the one-time mixed-doubles partner who'd tracked her down two years ago to let her know about a women's tennis-pro opening at a new country club in Modesto.

She could believe Therese, or she could trust her instincts about her friend.

Or she could pray.

She squeezed her eyes shut. *Jesus, tell me what to do.*

She lifted the phone to her ear. "Therese, I'll have to call you back."

&

The outer door clicked shut behind Ralph, and Jilly glared at the slump-shouldered man frowning back at her. "What are you doing here, and how did you know where to find me?"

"Therese suspended me. The cops are all over me. I didn't know where else to turn." Paul crossed the den and sank onto the edge of Harvey's sagging brown recliner. "You're the only person I could think of who knows beyond a doubt that I'd never use steroids, let alone push them on my students."

Jilly tapped her fingertips on her crossed arms. "Okay, that answered the first part of my question."

"I, uh, stalked your mailbox. Saw your landlady picking up your mail and readdressing it to forward."

"Paul—" Jilly started to chew him out about invasion of privacy until a new concern pricked her nerves. If Paul could so easily track her down—and if he really was innocent in the steroid scandal—then whoever had placed those threatening phone calls could locate her just as easily.

She reached for a glass of ice water on the end table and sipped slowly, trying to sort out her thoughts. "Okay," she began on a long exhalation, "tell me everything. Including what I walked in on in the men's room the day I broke my ankle."

Paul scraped a hand down his face. "I'd been suspicious for a couple of months that some of the boys were juicing. After class that day I followed them into the men's room, where I saw my prime suspect, Alex, doing some kind of deal with this other kid, Ted. Ted gave Alex some cash, and Alex handed Ted something that looked like a medicine vial. After Ted left, I confronted Alex, and that's when you walked in."

"Ted." Jilly released a whistling breath. "He's the guy who insisted I show him the Becker racquet."

"I'm so, so sorry, Jilly." He stared at her injured ankle and shook his head. "If I'd come forward sooner, I might have kept this from happening."

Images flashed through Jilly's thoughts—the men's room, the stepladder, the acne-faced kid. She raked her fingers through her hair in a vain attempt to untangle the confusion beneath her skull. "Why didn't you tell someone? Me. Therese. The cops. Why did you keep your suspicions to yourself?"

Paul lowered his chin to his chest. "Because of something else I didn't want anyone to find out about—especially you."

"Paul, we've been friends for years. What could be so bad that you didn't think you could tell me? So bad that you wouldn't report activity you *knew* was illegal?"

"Because I'm almost as guilty myself, and Alex knew about it." His voice fell to barely a whisper. "I'm fighting an addiction to pain pills."

A coldness seeped into Jilly's bones. Her gaze shifted sideways to the bottle of prescription pain relievers next to her water glass. "How? When?"

"Remember when I tore a shoulder muscle during our mixed-doubles game in the US Open qualifying round?"

Jilly nodded. "We were one game away from taking the match."

"Even after surgery and PT, the pain wouldn't go away. The doc tried to get me to wean off the pills, but hard as I've tried—more times than I can count—I haven't been able to kick them completely."

"So you've been getting them illegally?"

Paul's jaw muscles tensed. He flicked his gaze toward the floor. "Not *exactly*. I mean, I got legitimate doctors' prescriptions, but. . ." He gave a helpless shrug. "I won't bore you with the details."

Jilly had an overpowering urge to lunge off the sofa and pummel some sense into Paul's twisted brain. Only the bulky cast on her leg prevented it. She hugged her rib cage and took slow, deep breaths until she felt calm enough to speak. "Okay. What's done is done. But now you have to do the right thing. First, tell the cops everything you know about the steroids. Second, get yourself off those pain pills even if it means checking into rehab."

The macho tennis jock Jilly had known since college days vanished beneath Paul's shame-faced expression. He sent her a timid half smile. "That's why I came looking for you, Jilly. I knew I could count on my best friend to hold me accountable."

"Oh, believe me, now that you've hauled me kicking and screaming into the middle of this mess, I certainly will."

❧

On Thursday morning Cam scanned the church library shelves in search of the Tozer book he planned to refer to during his next prayer retreat. "Evelyn," he called to the librarian, "I can't find *The Pursuit of God*."

"Sounds like a spiritual problem to me." The plump redhead chuckled as she tapped her computer keyboard.

"Hah. Leave the jokes to the pastor."

Evelyn, who also happened to be the pastor's wife, rolled her eyes. "Who do you think supplies his sermon material?"

Cam sauntered over to the desk and peered at Evelyn's

computer monitor. She ran a finger down the onscreen list. "Sorry, Cam, the Tozer book is out on loan. Not due back for another week."

"Rats. The Bible college library didn't have any copies in either. Would you put my name on a waiting list and call me when it's returned?"

"Sure thing."

On his way to the parking lot, a lightness invaded Cam's steps. Hard as it had been to end things with Liz, he felt better about the decision with each passing day. And now, with nothing keeping him in town except a fat cat with litter box issues, he'd decided to return to the inn a day early for the next prayer retreat. Okay, so his reasons didn't entirely hinge upon enjoying the peaceful surroundings while he finished his preparations. Truth be told, he couldn't wait to see Jilly again.

And not simply out of concern for her state of mind.

No, ever since he'd picked her up at the Kansas City airport, she'd been inching her way into his heart. Or maybe expanding the portion he'd kept reserved for her all these years without even realizing it. A lot had happened in both their lives since they were kids. Unpredictable circumstances had sent them down vastly different paths. And yet here they were, together again and surely not by coincidence. Cam had to believe God had a hand in bringing Jilly back to Blossom Hills. And now, more than ever, he prayed he could help Jilly come to terms with her past and her future—and, God willing, convince her that her future could be right here with Cam.

Arriving at the inn, he parked the Mariner near the front entrance. He scooped up his soft-sided briefcase full of books and notes, looped his arm through the handle of a sack of bakery goodies, and grabbed his travel bag from the backseat. He jogged up the porch steps and peered through the beveled-glass doors, hoping Jilly wouldn't be at the front desk this time of day. She didn't expect him until tomorrow, and he wanted to surprise her.

No sign of her in the lobby. He slipped inside and listened. Voices drifted down the broad staircase—probably the housecleaning crew. The door to Harvey's office was open, and a quick glance told Cam Jilly wasn't working there either. If she obeyed doctor's orders—not to mention Harvey's and Cam's—she should be in the family quarters taking it easy.

He dropped his briefcase and travel bag by the front desk and started down the short corridor with the bag of baked goods. As he lifted his hand to knock on the door, a peal of laughter burst from the inn kitchen. He'd know Jilly's bubbly laugh anywhere, and the sound of it made his heart zing. He reversed direction and headed across the lobby.

As he neared the door to the kitchen, an unfamiliar male voice drew him up short. "And remember the time you back-pedaled to go for that overhand smash and fell smack on top of the ball boy?"

"Poor kid was probably scarred for life." Jilly's voice shook with mirth.

"No kidding." The guy again. "Hey, are there any more of these macadamia nut cookies? They're great."

"The tall canister on the counter."

"Can I bring you anything?"

"Anything but those. You know me and macadamia nuts. How about a chocolate-chip from the other cookie jar?"

Cam peered around the door frame to see Jilly and a muscled blond guy nibbling on giant cookies. When the guy reached across the table to flick a crumb from Jilly's chin, Cam's stomach bottomed out.

He glanced down at the bag he carried. It contained a half-dozen apple fritters, the thick, doughy kind Jilly used to gorge herself on as a kid. His gut twisted. Suddenly Liz's bouts of jealousy seemed downright tame.

twelve

Jilly slapped Paul's hand away from her chin. As she reached for a napkin, she glimpsed Cam standing in the doorway, and her breath snagged. Her mouth spread into a surprised grin. "Hey, guy! Guess we were talking and laughing so much that I didn't hear the door chime. What are you doing here? Did I get my days mixed up?"

"Decided to come out a day early." His voice carried an unpleasant edge. The look on his face made Jilly's stomach tighten.

Paul rose and stepped around the table. "Just a wild guess. You must be Cameron Lane." He thrust out his hand. "I'm Paul Edgar. Jilly's been talking about you ever since I got here."

"Paul. Jilly's told me about you, too." Cam stared at Paul's outstretched hand a microsecond longer than seemed polite. When he finally took it, his jaw knotted. He glanced toward Jilly, confusion narrowing his eyes.

Of course. Unless Cam had talked to Harvey since last night, he'd be wondering why Paul had shown up here, especially after Jilly had shared her suspicions about the men's room incident and the threatening calls. And if he'd been standing there very long, he had to have heard them laughing together as if nothing was wrong.

She positioned the walker in front of her and pushed off the chair. "Finish your cookie, Paul. I'll just go get Cam checked in."

Cam waved stiff fingers. "No rush."

"It's okay. I could use the walker practice." She started for the door. As she passed Cam, a whiff of something sweet and delicious filled her nostrils. Childhood memories burst upon her brain like a bite into a tender, juicy baked apple.

Fritters! She flipped her head around and spied the small white bag Cam carried, definitely the source of the tantalizing aroma. She grinned at Cam, then nodded toward the bag. "Anything in there for me?"

"As a matter of fact." The rigid lines around his mouth slowly eased. "I was driving by Ruth Hartford's bakery and out of the blue it came to me that you used to love apple fritters."

"Still do. Ruth Hartford, the lady from your first retreat?"

"Yep. Her daughter runs the bakery now. You remember Ruth?"

Jilly grimaced. "Hard to forget someone who kept trying to. . ." *Okay, let's stop right there.* No sense embarrassing herself further with reference to the Hartfords' utterly unsubtle attempts at matchmaking.

She edged behind the front desk and scooted onto the barstool, then shoved the walker aside and reached for a registration card. "One deluxe suite for Mr. Lane."

Cam chuckled. "Since when do I rate the deluxe suite?"

"Since you brought me apple fritters, naturally." Jilly handed him a room key and smiled up expectantly.

He slid the bag toward her with a lopsided grin that turned her insides doughy. "All yours, Miss Gardner."

Glancing toward the kitchen, Jilly remembered Paul. Her smile faded as she looked up at Cam. "I guess you're wondering what Paul's doing here."

He leaned his elbows on the counter and tipped his head in the direction of the kitchen. His face hardened again. "So what's the deal?"

Jilly slid a fritter out of the bag and broke it in half. "Here, share this with me and I'll explain."

❧

Steroids. Cam's gut clenched. The three bites of apple fritter he'd swallowed rose on a wave of bile. He wanted to feel relief that Paul Edgar was only a friend, not a serious romantic interest for Jilly. He wanted to thank God for saving Jilly from anything more serious than a broken ankle because of Paul's stupidity and cowardice.

But all he could think about was Terrance. All he could see was Terrance's swollen, acne-pitted face. All he could hear were his mother's terrified sobs when she discovered her younger son dead in their basement rec room, the result of a steroid-induced heart attack.

And Jilly was taking Paul Edgar's side. She'd given him a room here at the inn. She'd sat there in the kitchen, laughing with him and eating cookies as if Paul's turning a blind eye to steroid use and abusing oxycodone were no big deal.

"Cam?" Jilly's concerned voice sliced through his angry thoughts. "Cam, you look furious. What's wrong?"

"What's *wrong*?" His knotted fist beat a slow rhythm on the countertop. He slid his gaze toward the kitchen, then whipped it back to Jilly. "What's wrong is you're harboring a criminal and acting like it's perfectly fine."

Jilly stiffened. "It is *not* perfectly fine. And for the record, Paul is not a criminal. He's a friend, and I'm trying to help him. Harvey gave me the name of a lawyer who can get Paul straight with the Modesto police. And in the meantime," she continued with a huff, "I was hoping my other friend—namely you—might have some professional contacts who could help Paul get off the drugs."

Her pointed words bled off some of Cam's anger. He scrubbed the back of his head. "Sorry, I overreacted."

"No, you didn't. I know where you're coming from." She dipped her chin. Her voice dropped a notch. "Last night Harvey told me about Terrance. Cam, I'm so sorry. I never realized his death was due to steroid abuse."

"My parents did their best to keep it quiet. Not many people knew." *But I should have. I was his big brother, closer to him than anyone. If only I'd recognized the signs, I could have done something.*

Jilly's tone softened even more. She reached across the counter to touch his elbow. "Harvey says you've never really gotten over it."

The feel of her fingertips drew his entire focus. His lungs refused to function. He didn't want to think about Terrance or Paul or the prayer retreat. "Jilly, I—"

"Hey, y'all." Paul.

Great timing. Cam jerked his arm off the counter and turned to face the blond tennis jock. He struggled for an impassive expression.

"Sorry, didn't mean to interrupt." Paul stuffed his hands into his jeans pockets. "There's a delivery guy at the kitchen entrance asking where to put stuff."

"Oh, boy." Jilly hopped off the barstool and grabbed her walker. "That's the food for this weekend. And Heather left early today because of a dentist appointment."

Cam pulled himself together and started for the kitchen. "I can get there faster than you. What do I tell the guy?"

"Cold stuff in the fridge, everything else on the table. I'm right behind you to help put it all away."

"I can help, too." Paul jogged up beside Cam. "Might as well make myself useful."

Cam cut him a sidelong glance. Behind them, Cam heard the chimes as someone entered through the front door. He paused to see a young couple breeze in with luggage in tow. They approached Jilly just as she rounded the front desk.

"Oh, you must be the Wyatts. Your room's all ready." Jilly waved Cam on. "Be there in a few minutes. I need to get these folks checked in."

Cam nodded and continued to the kitchen. He showed the deliveryman where to put things, then got started sorting the groceries. Paul pitched in, doing a fair job of figuring out what went where, considering the muscle-bound, drug-addicted jerk probably knew his way around a tennis court way better than a kitchen.

Get a grip, Lane. Give the guy the benefit of the doubt, why don't you? For Jilly's sake if for no other reason.

Paul shifted a ten-pound bag of rice from one hand to the other. "I take it Jilly filled you in on my situation?"

"Yep." Cam studied the label on a jar of Kalamata olives. *"Serving size, 5 olives. Calories per serving, 45." Might need to know that someday.*

"I never meant to get her involved. It's just. . .I didn't know where else to go."

"Right. Since you're friends and all." Garbanzo beans. *"Total carbs, 45 grams. Dietary fiber, 12 grams." Important stuff on product labels.*

"I just want you to know, I'm gonna get clean and get this mess straightened out."

"Good." Cam tucked several jars and cans between his forearms and chest and stalked to the pantry.

"She's crazy about you, by the way."

Four cans of garbanzo beans hit the tile floor with an ear-splitting crash.

❧

"What on earth is going on in here?" Jilly hobbled over to where Cam stood amid a tumble of dented vegetable cans.

"I. . .uh. . ."

"Dropped something. Yeah, I noticed." She tried to read the look on his face. He seemed a lot more shook up than he should be after dropping a few bean cans. "You okay?"

"Here, let me." Paul rushed over and started grabbing up cans. "Didn't drop any on your foot, did you? That would hurt."

"No. No, I'm fine." Cam stepped over a can and shoved an olive jar onto the pantry shelf. He turned and stared at Jilly as if he wanted to say something but couldn't figure out how.

Paul ducked past Cam and set the cans in the pantry. "I should go give that lawyer another call. Hopefully he's talked to the Modesto police by now." Seconds later he vanished in the direction of the lobby.

A kitchen chair sat nearby. Jilly scooted toward it and plopped down with a groan. "Cam, if you're going to give me another chewing-out about trusting Paul—"

"That's not it." Cam lifted his hands in a helpless gesture before sinking onto the chair facing her. He sighed. Laced and unlaced his fingers.

Jilly tried to be patient and let him find whatever words he searched for, but his edginess had her worried. Did he have something else to get off his chest, maybe something more about how his brother died? She couldn't believe she'd never known Terrance had OD'd on steroids. Poor Cam, carrying that grief all these years, and then to be confronted with the issue all over again when Paul showed up—

"Did Harvey say anything to you about Liz and me?"

The question blew through her brain like a sudden gust of wind. "What?"

"I said, did Harvey—"

"I heard the question. I'm just trying to change gears here." Jilly rubbed her temple. As his words penetrated, her stomach somersaulted, then plummeted to her toes. Cam and Liz were getting married. What else could it be? He'd thought things through, gotten over his commitment phobia, and popped the question.

Disappointment assaulted her. Disappointment she had no right to feel.

She willed her mouth into some semblance of a smile and blinked away a sudden spurt of tears. "Oh, Cam, I'm so happy for you. Sorry, these allergies. . ." She groped for a tissue in her pocket and blew her nose. "Have you set the date? I bet that little boy is so excited to be getting a new dad."

It slowly dawned on her that Cam was staring openmouthed, one eyebrow arched as if she'd grown two heads. He straightened, his lips twisting into a crooked grin. "What are you talking about?"

"You and Liz. Isn't that what—" His bemused expression told her they'd experienced a major disconnect. She wadded the tissue and dabbed away the trickle beneath her left eye. "You and Liz, you're not engaged?"

"How many ways do I have to tell you? There is nothing between Liz and me." He took her hand in his and inched closer. His tone mellowed. "I thought Harvey might have told you already. Liz and I are no longer seeing each other. It's over."

His touch seared her palm. Her voice squeaked out. "Over?"

"As much as anything that never really amounted to much can be called *over*." His thumb raked across her knuckles. He kept his eyes lowered. "Jilly, I'm feeling like there could be something between you and me. Am I crazy?"

Surely he could hear her thudding heart, feel the pulse throbbing beneath his fingertips. Words log-jammed in her throat. Any second now her chest would explode.

He lifted hazel eyes full of questions. "Jilly?"

He'd spoken the words she'd imagined hearing from his lips almost since the day he hefted her luggage off the carousel at the Kansas City airport—since she was a string-bean preteen with a king-size crush, if truth be told. A fizzy, fuzzy sensation swirled around her head. "I feel something for you, too, Cam. I just didn't think we had a chance."

"Because of Liz?"

"Liz. . .and a whole lot of other things." Like the fact that she hadn't planned on sticking around Blossom Hills indefinitely. Like the fact that she couldn't let go of the hope of rehabilitating her ankle and resuming her tennis career, or at least coaching if she never made it back on the pro circuit.

"I know I've kind of sprung this on you." Cam's knee brushed hers. "But I was hoping we could see where things go."

She sighed. Maybe she should stop worrying about the future and enjoy the possibilities of *now*. "Yeah. I think I'd like that."

He'd like to cancel the prayer retreat this weekend and spend some time alone with Jilly. Unfortunately, five couples from the young marrieds Sunday school class would show up in less than four hours.

Last night had been interesting. The couple who'd arrived at the same time as the grocery delivery turned out to be newlyweds on their honeymoon trip. As the inn's only midweek guests, they earned special attention, including a candlelight dinner served by Heather, followed by dessert and coffee on the deck as the sun set behind the hills. They concluded their evening with a moonlight row across the lake, courtesy of Ralph wearing a cheesy black-and-white-striped gondolier's outfit.

Cam and Jilly had secretly watched from the office window until Harvey arrived and chided them for spying. His harangue held little bite, however. The glint in his eye suggested he rather liked the idea of Cam and Jilly sharing the romantic view.

Cam rather liked it himself.

And he liked the view before him this morning. Jilly sat on her barstool behind the front desk, a half-eaten apple in one hand, a ballpoint pen flicking back and forth in the other. She bent over a checklist of some sort, probably something to do with the retreat guests. A pretty pout pushed out her lower lip. Her tongue flicked out to catch a dribble of apple juice.

She looked up suddenly and smiled. "How long have you been standing there?"

"Long enough to wish I could break free from the group this evening and borrow Ralph's gondolier shirt."

"Oh? And why's that?"

"So I could row you across the lake, and we could watch the stars together."

A sultry laugh burbled from Jilly's throat. Using the end

of the pen, she tucked that curvy lock of hair behind her ear. "Mr. Lane. You've been spending too much time around our honeymooners."

"Since they're staying through the weekend, I was thinking about inviting them to join the retreat. What do you think?"

She arched an eyebrow. "I hope you're kidding."

"What, you don't think they'd go for the idea?" He feigned a disbelieving frown.

The couple in question strolled in the back door. Jilly shot Cam a warning glance before greeting the newlyweds. "How was your hike? Did you find the waterfall I told you about?"

"It was gorgeous," the new Mrs. Wyatt answered. "We considered getting lost up there, but James was too worried about missing lunch." She flicked a starry-eyed, if somewhat frustrated, glance at her groom.

"That chef of yours is amazing." James's face seemed to have frozen in the permanent grin of a typical honeymooner. He gazed lovingly at his wife. "Allison, maybe you could ask Heather for some pointers."

The remark earned him a slug to the solar plexus. Forget the prayer retreat—this couple might be better served by some preemptive marriage counseling.

"Don't worry, you're back in plenty of time for lunch." Jilly reached for a note by the phone. "Oh, and I confirmed your dinner theater reservation for this evening. Doors open at seven, so you'll want to leave here no later than six-fifteen."

"Great, thanks." James slid his arm around Allison's waist. "How long until lunch?"

Jilly checked her watch. "At least forty-five minutes. In the meantime, there's fresh iced tea and appetizers around the corner in the lounge."

The Wyatts smiled and excused themselves. Cam noticed they bypassed the lounge entrance and went straight upstairs.

Yep, honeymooners.

He stole a glance at Jilly. Could she ever love him like that? Did she wonder, as he did, if their mutual attraction could someday lead to a lifetime commitment?

thirteen

At the sound of voices, Jilly looked up from the office computer to see Cam leading his retreat group through the lobby. They'd just finished lunch, and for their afternoon session Ralph had set up extra chairs on the deck. Two of the wives were visibly pregnant, which meant sprawling on blankets under the trees was out of the question. Not to mention the necessity of a ladies' room nearby.

Jilly chuckled, but as she heard them step through the back door onto the deck, a subtle urging tugged at her heart. Cam had told her several times she was welcome to sit in on any of his sessions, but until now she'd resisted. She and God still had a few issues to work out.

Fingertips fidgeting on the computer keyboard, she watched the couples find seats around the circle. The fathers-to-be took the less comfortable plastic deck chairs, helping their wives into the adirondacks. A couple of the other guys sparred good-naturedly for a mesh lounge. The huskier of the two finally won out. Jilly hoped the mesh would hold him.

Cam started speaking, his words muffled by the window glass. The tug in Jilly's spirit grew stronger. She hopped around to the other side of the desk and eased open the sash.

". . .so what I'd like to focus on this afternoon," Cam was saying, "is how our prayer life is directly affected by how we see God. If you think of Him as judge or lawgiver, your approach in prayer is going to be much different from the person who looks to God as a loving Father."

"I know what you're saying," one of the wives said. "My dad died when I was very young, so I didn't grow up with a strong father figure. It took years before I could think of God as a Father who loved me unconditionally."

Jilly scooted onto the corner of the desk. Yeah, she could relate. She had no idea who her real father was. Her birth certificate listed him as "unknown," and information she'd gleaned from case workers suggested any one of her mother's several male acquaintances could have been her father, none of whom seemed worthy of the title.

As for her mother, she'd never managed to stay off the booze long enough to figure out this whole parenting thing. Eventually a social worker convinced her to terminate her parental rights.

Jilly returned her attention to the conversation outside as one of the husbands said, "I didn't become a Christian until a couple of years ago. Not really, anyway. My parents always took me to church, but the preacher was one of those fire-and-brimstone types. Scared me so bad, I wanted nothing to do with Christianity." He draped an arm around his pregnant wife's shoulders. "At least until Kathy got hold of me and helped me see God in a new light."

Jilly could thank Harvey and Alice for showing her what genuine parental love really was. And for teaching her about the love of God. A pained sigh rippled through her chest. If only she'd trusted them. If only she'd trusted God. She might have spared herself and the Nelsons a decade of heartache.

Paul sidled into the office. "Hey, Jilly, you busy?"

"Just checking on the group outside." She closed the window and swiveled to face him. "What's up?"

"Needed somebody to talk to." He collapsed into a chair, hands knotted between his knees. His futile efforts to stifle the withdrawal tremors tore at Jilly's heart.

She edged around the desk and settled into her chair. "You staying off the pain meds?"

"Yeah, but it's tough. Man, I don't know if I can do this." He exhaled sharply. His glance moved to the pill bottle next to Jilly's water glass. A hungry look flattened his lips. "Be careful with those, that's all I can say."

"Believe me, I am." She'd already cut back on the dose as much as she could bear. Enduring a little discomfort now seemed far preferable to fighting addiction later. She slid her hand toward the pill bottle and swept it into the desk drawer. Out of sight, out of mind. *Maybe.* "Try to hang in there until Monday. Cam promised he'd take you to get help."

"Yeah. So talk to me. Please." Paul inched lower in the chair, nervous fingers drumming on his thighs. Sweat beaded his upper lip. "Tell me more about this Cam guy. He seems cool."

"Like I told you, he's an old friend from when I grew up here."

"That line didn't fool me the first time you used it, and I'm not buying it today. You two have a whole lot more than friendship going on."

Jilly snatched up a pen and doodled on a scratch pad. "Maybe. But we're taking time to get to know each other again."

Paul sprang from the chair and paced between the desk and a row of filing cabinets. "What's he gonna do when you go back to Modesto? Long-distance relationships are the pits."

An imaginary knife blade carved a hole in Jilly's midsection. Since her fall down the deck steps she'd been trying not to think too far ahead. Part of her desperately hoped a few months of rehabilitation would put her back on the tennis courts, at least in some capacity. Another part—a part that grew stronger each day—made her want to wrap her arms around Cameron Lane and never let go.

Couldn't she have it both ways? *God, are You listening?*

Paul halted in front of her and jammed his hands into his pockets. He nodded toward the window. "So what's with all this prayer stuff? You think it does any good?"

Jilly's head popped up. *Did she?* "I'd like to believe it does."

"Cam seems like a smart guy." Paul began pacing again. He drew the back of his hand across his mouth. "He told me last night I should ask God to help me through this. So after I went up to my room, I sorta prayed. At least I think I was praying. Never really tried it before."

A funny, tickly feeling started under Jilly's breastbone—a twinge of conviction mixed with exhilaration. She pulled her walker closer and stood. "You know, I'm a bit rusty in the prayer department, too. How about we go sit in on Cam's afternoon session?"

❧

"Before we move on, does anyone else—" Cam twisted his head around at the sound of footsteps and the unmistakable *clunk-creak* of Jilly's walker.

"Sorry to interrupt." Jilly cast him a sheepish grin. "Paul and I thought we'd join you if it's okay."

"Sure." Cam stood to enlarge the circle and drew up a couple more chairs. He made sure Jilly took the one immediately to his left, although when his pulse kicked into a higher gear, he gave serious thought to the wisdom of having her so close.

He cleared his throat and took his seat. "Everyone, you remember Jilly. She's the gal who checked you in yesterday. And this is her friend Paul Edgar."

"Hi again, Jilly," said Roy, the man on Cam's right. "How long have you and Cam been married?"

The turkey wrap Cam had for lunch sprouted feathers and wings. A quick glance in Jilly's direction revealed a blush creeping up her neck.

One of the pregnant ladies caught Cam's eye and winked. "Obviously Roy and Cheryl are new at Covenant. Cam is a confirmed bachelor."

"Yikes, my bad." Roy grimaced. "I just assumed from the way you two were making eyes at each other at dinner last night. . ."

His wife nudged him. "Honey, you're embarrassing them."

"A*hem.*" Cam doused the flames heating his own face with a swig from his water bottle. He plopped open his Bible. "Let's get back on topic, shall we?"

Doing so proved more challenging than he'd expected. . .or maybe not. While he attempted to steer the discussion toward various forms of prayer, he found himself continually distracted by Paul's fidgeting. The poor guy would cross one leg, then the other, twiddle his thumbs, rake fingers through his hair. The other couples grew more and more unfocused, as well.

Finally Jilly reached over and rested a hand on Paul's arm, holding it there until he stilled. "Maybe this wasn't such a good idea," she whispered. "Cam, I'm sorry. We shouldn't have intruded."

A still, small voice told Cam otherwise. "No, stay. I'm glad you joined us. Paul, would you mind if I tell the group a little more about you?" With his eyes he tried to convey his intention to be tactful.

Paul's knees jumped up and down. "Okay, I guess."

Addressing the group, Cam said, "Without going into details, let me just say Paul is struggling with a substance abuse problem. I only met him a couple of days ago, so we really don't know each other. What I do know is that he came here because he knew he could count on his friend Jilly for help, which plays right into the whole subject of prayer. Christ is the one true friend we can always turn to, whatever problems we face."

A chorus of murmured responses sounded throughout the circle: "Amen." "So true."

"And just as we approach our heavenly Father in various ways—through the Psalms, intercessory prayer, thanksgiving, worship—we need to be open to the different ways He comes to us. One very tangible way is through other human beings, imperfect as they are." Cam shifted his gaze to Jilly and offered a gentle smile. "Sometimes the answer to a prayer is as near as the friend sitting next to us."

❧

By the time the session ended, Jilly couldn't wait to get back inside. Despite the pleasant warmth of the afternoon sun, something in the air had completely blocked her sinuses and turned her eyelids into sandpaper. The package with her allergy prescription had yet to arrive, and every time she thought to call Denise to ask about it, something else distracted her.

While Paul went to the kitchen for a caffeine hit, she hurried to her room—as much of a hurry as she could manage with the walker—and pawed through her purse in search of her cell phone. She carried it across the hall to the den and sank into Harvey's recliner, then flipped open the phone and scrolled for Denise's number.

Moments later her landlady answered. "Jilly! Are you still in Missouri? How are you?"

"A little worse for wear. I hurt my ankle again and had to have surgery."

"Oh, honey, how'd you do that?"

"Long story. I'll tell you later." Jilly reached for a tissue and dabbed her drippy nose. "What I really need is my allergy meds. Did they ever come?"

"I found the package on your doorstep just yesterday. I took it straight to the UPS store to have it forwarded."

"Thank goodness!" Jilly whooshed out a thankful breath.

"Looks like it got lost in transit somewhere. The box was pretty beat-up."

"At least it's on its way. Everything else okay there?"

"Finally got my new sprinkler system installed. Oh, and I'm thinking about getting a burglar alarm. The neighborhood watch committee sent out a flyer the other day about possible prowlers."

An unexplained niggling started at the base of Jilly's neck. Then she remembered Paul had found out where Jilly was by watching her mailbox. She'd have to rag him about getting her neighbors all riled up. With a casual laugh, she said, "Our neighborhood has always been very safe. I'm sure they're just being overly cautious."

"Maybe. But Stanley next door told me he's seen suspicious-looking vehicles cruising the block. As single women we can't be too careful."

"I guess not." No point in saying anything about Paul. His mailbox snooping may have been unlawful but no real harm had been done.

"So when do you think you'll be home, honey?"

Jilly squeezed her itchy eyes shut and exhaled through tense lips. "I don't know how to tell you this, Denise, but I'm not even sure I'm coming back to Modesto. At least not to stay."

Denise gasped. "Why ever not?"

As Jilly explained about her fall down the deck steps and the depressing prognosis concerning her future in tennis, her eyes brimmed with tears. "It was the job at Silverheels that brought me to Modesto in the first place. If I can't continue coaching, I'm seriously considering staying here in Blossom Hills."

"I know you have family there and all, but I'd sure miss you."

Family. Yes indeed, Jilly had family here, and the reminder brought renewed comfort. *Thank You, Lord.* "I'd miss you, too, Denise. You've been a great friend and a wonderful landlady." She sucked in a quick breath. "But nothing's settled yet. By summer's end I should have a better idea about my plans."

"All right then. I'll keep forwarding your mail. Do stay in touch, though."

"I will, I promise."

As they said their good-byes, a knock sounded on the outer door. Jilly clicked her phone shut. "It's open. Come on in."

The squeak of rubber-soled sneakers sounded in the hall, followed by Cam's appearance in the den doorway. "You okay? I could tell your allergies were kicking in big-time out there."

"I'm out of meds. My landlady finally forwarded my prescription yesterday, but of course it'll be a few more days before it gets here."

Cam propped a hip against the door frame. "Isn't there anything over the counter you can take?"

"Nothing works as well as my prescription."

"Why don't you call your doctor and have him phone in something to a pharmacy here? Harvey could pick it up on his way home from visiting Alice."

Jilly brightened momentarily, then her shoulders drooped. "It's Saturday. The doctor's office won't even be open."

"He has a service, doesn't he? When you explain your situation, I'm sure they can get a prescription called in."

Jilly reached for her cell phone again. "I'll need to give them a pharmacy number. Got any recommendations?"

A frown flickered across Cam's face. He shrugged. "I always use Riley's. One of the pharmacists there goes to my church. And it would be on Harvey's way from the rehab hospital."

"Okay, I'm desperate enough to try anything." She sniffled and blew her nose while Cam jotted the number on the back of a magazine she handed him. Interesting that he knew a pharmacy number so well he didn't have to look it up. Cam didn't look the type to have that many health problems.

The doctor's answering service promised to have someone return her call within the hour. She cradled the phone in her lap and smiled up at Cam. "Wish I'd thought of this days ago. With any luck I'll be breathing again by evening."

"Great. Breathing is always a good thing." His eyes softened, and Jilly's heart rate kicked up a notch.

She crumpled her damp tissue. "Don't you need to get back to your retreat?"

"We're taking a thirty-minute break. I was worried about you."

"I'm fine. I'm just going to sit here with my feet up for a

while and maybe try a cool washcloth on these allergy eyes."
Wow. She must look really appealing with her drippy nose
and swollen lids.

"Here, let me." Cam scurried to the bathroom and returned
with a damp cloth. "Want a pillow under your ankle? Need
some water? A soda?"

"Please, I'm not an—" She started to say *invalid.* All right,
so she basically was one. She gave a self-conscious laugh and
allowed herself to wallow in the attention as Cam helped
her get settled. "Careful there, you could spoil a girl with this
kind of treatment."

He grinned. "I aim to please."

fourteen

Of all the weekends Cam had to schedule a prayer retreat, why did it have to be this one? Surrounded by all these happily married young couples gushing over each other, all he could think about was Jilly. When he'd left her earlier, with that cast on her ankle, her eyes practically swollen shut, and a red nose to rival Rudolph's, she'd looked so enticingly vulnerable. He'd like to send the retreat couples packing—or maybe up to their rooms for some married R & R—and spend the rest of the weekend taking care of Jilly.

The last session of the afternoon finally wrapped up, and Cam followed the couples down the broad staircase from the second-floor conference room. As he crossed the lobby, Harvey swept in through the back door.

"Hey, Cam, how's our girl? I picked up the meds from Riley's."

Cam signaled his group into the dining room, where spicy garlic and tomato aromas beckoned. *Hope the couples packed mouthwash.* "Last time I checked, Jilly was taking a nap in your recliner. Probably the best thing for her right now."

"Poor thing. Always did have a terrible time with hay fever. I'd hoped—"

The front door burst open, and a UPS delivery person strode to the front desk. "Got an overnight package for a Ms. Jillian Gardner, care of the Dogwood Blossom Inn."

Harvey set the pharmacy bag on the desk and stepped forward. "That's my daughter. I'll take it."

Admiration warmed Cam's chest. Harvey hadn't hesitated for even a second. Jilly *was* his daughter in every way that counted.

The UPS man handed Harvey a small box, tapped some keys on his handheld tracking computer, and scurried out.

Cam peered over Harvey's shoulder at the shipping label. "Denise Moran from Modesto—that's Jilly's landlady, isn't it? Maybe it's the prescription Jilly was waiting on. She didn't think it would get here before next week."

Harvey chuckled. "Good, then she ought to be well stocked for a while. That Liz gal at Riley's personally made sure the prescription was ready and waiting when I got there."

Cam's stomach clenched. "Liz was working today?"

"Said she recognized Jillian's name when the doctor's call came in." Harvey tucked both packages under his arm. "Best get these to Jillian. The sooner she gets her medicine down, the faster she'll start feeling better."

Watching Harvey disappear through the door to the family quarters, Cam could only imagine Liz's awkwardness at having to handle Jilly's prescription. He still felt horrible for the pain he caused Liz with the breakup. She was a good person, a good mother, and she didn't deserve to be hurt. But neither did she—nor Sammy—deserve the false hope of a future that simply wasn't going to happen.

❧

On Monday morning, Jilly stood before the bathroom mirror and inhaled through a completely clear nose. Man, it felt good to breathe again! She glanced at the two prescription bottles sitting side by side on the counter. That Denise— what an angel for going to the trouble and expense of overnight shipping. Jilly had noted the cost on the shipping label, and first thing Sunday morning she wrote out a check and a heartfelt thank-you note to mail to her landlady.

"Jillian, you up?"

"'Morning, Harvey. Come on in."

"Thought I heard you stirring around." Harvey leaned in the bathroom doorway and grinned at her reflection in the mirror. "Cam's in the lobby with Paul. They're ready to head to town anytime. You still planning on going along?"

"I'll be ready in a sec. And once we get Paul set up with a rehab counselor, I'd like to visit Alice."

"She'll be so glad to see you. Tell her I'll be by later this afternoon."

Jilly ran a comb through her hair and applied some lip gloss, then grabbed her walker and followed Harvey out to the lobby.

"Hey, gorgeous." Cam ambled over and tucked a strand of her hair behind her ear, his touch raising goose bumps on her neck. "I can actually see those big brown eyes of yours this morning."

Jilly snickered. "And I can actually see out of them."

"I parked near the front steps. Are you sure you can manage them okay with that contraption?"

"Are you kidding? I'm getting to be an old pro." She wouldn't admit that the hardest part of going anywhere was maneuvering the stupid walker. But what choice did she have, other than plopping her rear into a wheelchair and allowing someone else to chauffeur her around? The walker may be cumbersome, but at least it spared her bruised ribs while giving her a semblance of independence.

Although, when she looked into Cam's warm gaze, independence seemed slightly overrated. Which was why she didn't argue when he suggested they bring the wheelchair along "just in case."

Within the hour, they sat with Paul in the waiting room of New Life Addiction Recovery Center. Jilly didn't like what she saw in Paul's face. Even though the lawyer had gotten Paul off the hook with the Modesto police, four days off the pain pills had left him shaky and pale. He edged lower in the gray tweed chair and leaned his head against the wall.

Jilly reached across the magazine-strewn side table and touched his arm. "It's going to be okay. Hang in there."

Paul slid bloodshot eyes in her direction and gave a weak nod.

An inner door opened and a stocky, bearded man stepped through. "Come on back, Paul. I'm Ed Huttar. I'll be your counselor."

A glimmer of panic widened Paul's eyes. He stood and groped for Jilly's hand. "Keep saying those prayers for me, okay? That's all that's holding me together right now."

"You bet." Jilly pulled herself up with her walker and gave Paul a reassuring smile before he trudged through the door with the counselor.

Cam tucked an arm around her shoulder. "I've known Ed for years. Paul couldn't be in better hands."

"It just hurts to see Paul go through this. I've known him for years, too."

"Like he said, we'll keep praying for him." He gave her shoulder a squeeze and started for the exit. "You ready to visit Alice?"

She blew out a noisy breath and pushed the walker forward. "Let's go."

❧

Jilly and Cam arrived at the rehab hospital in time to watch Alice complete the cooldown portion of her cardiac exercise class. Her face glowed with renewed health as she grinned at them from the treadmill. A nurse beckoned Alice over to a chair and gave her a few minutes to rest before taking a blood pressure reading.

"Looking good, Mrs. Nelson. You're free until after lunch." The nurse turned to a computer to type in some information.

Rising, Alice gave an exaggerated sigh. "*Free* is a relative term around here. Real freedom is when you let me go home."

The nurse laughed. "At the rate you're improving, I'm sure that'll be very soon."

Alice reached for a towel and patted the beads of perspiration from her forehead as she worked her way between the rows of treadmills and exercise bikes to reach Jilly and Cam. "Aren't you two a welcome sight? Want to join me for some fruit juice?"

"Love to." Waves of warmth bathed Jilly's limbs as she leaned across the walker to receive Alice's hug. How she'd missed the firm grip of those arms, the caress of a mother's cheek.

Her throat tightened on a choked sob. She sniffed back unexpected tears.

"Honey?" Alice drew back, brows knitted. "What is it?"

Jilly thumbed away the wetness beneath her eyes. "Nothing, nothing at all."

Her gaze still on Jilly, Alice tucked her arm beneath Cam's. "Cam, the snack bar is just down the hall. Would you be a sweetie and go fetch us some drinks?"

Cam shot Jilly a worried look of his own. "Sure, Alice, glad to. What would you like?"

"I could go for a cranberry juice. How about you, Jilly?"

She shrugged. "Sounds fine."

Alice pointed Cam in the direction of the snack bar and said they'd meet him in the atrium. As they started toward the corridor, she murmured something else to Cam that Jilly couldn't hear.

Falling into step beside Alice, she matched the older woman's shuffling pace—not difficult to do with the cumbersome walker. "Care to tell me what that was all about?"

Alice cast her an achingly familiar smile of understanding. "Just told him to take his time. Thought maybe you could use some woman-to-woman talk."

A shiver started in Jilly's belly. It wasn't merely woman-to-woman conversation she needed. What she craved was motherly advice.

In the atrium they found a quiet corner near a potted palm. Jilly sank onto a bamboo love seat with hibiscus-print cushions and shoved the walker to one side.

Alice nudged a footstool over for Jilly's ankle, then settled next to her, tucking one leg under the other in a girlish pose. "Now tell me, how's my girl? How are you *really* doing, honey?"

"Oh, Alice, I'm confused about so many things. My whole life is one big mess."

Alice enfolded Jilly's hand in her own. "I know Harvey and I had a lot to do with your confusion. I'm so terribly sorry for the pain we've caused you."

"Now that I know the truth about why you didn't adopt me, I. . .well, I'm doing my best to understand."

"And do you understand that you truly are our daughter? Always have been and always will be?" Alice's grip tightened. Her voice grew firm with resolve. "No judge's decree or adoption certificate could make us love you any more than we already do."

"I know that now. I guess I've always known it deep inside—in here." Jilly touched her breastbone and blinked back tears.

Alice flicked away a trickle from her own cheek. "Then you forgive us?"

"Of course I do." A ragged sigh tore through Jilly's throat. "I'm just so sorry for the lost years."

They shared a long, healing hug, then chuckled at each other's weepiness. Jilly composed herself with a slow, deep breath. "Wow, I haven't cried this much in I don't know how long."

"You never were one to give in to tears. Always so brave and stoic."

"Yeah, and look where that got me." Jilly flicked her hair away from her face. "I think that's part of why I'm so confused lately. I don't know what to do with all these emotions."

Alice offered a shy smile. "And do any of these emotions have to do with a certain young man of our acquaintance?"

"If you mean Cam, then. . .yes." Jilly shuddered and tucked

her hands between her knees. "Alice, I'm terrified. Even before a major tournament I was never this nervous."

"But what's to be afraid of? It's pretty clear he's smitten with you, too." Alice quirked a brow. "Has been since you were kids, if I'm any judge of true love."

At the word *love*, Jilly jerked her head around. "Do you think so?"

"I do."

"But I was so flaky then, a self-centered tennis brat."

Alice chuckled. "I'm pretty sure that isn't the way Cam saw you."

"Well, at least I'm not naive little Jillian Gardner anymore." Regret congested her throat. "I wanted so much to be someone different, so badly that after I left for college, I even quit going by the name Jillian."

"And I understand why." Alice patted her arm. "But who you are is not dependent on what name you're called. It's who you believe yourself to be. It's who God created you to be."

Thoughts of romance temporarily banished, Jilly stared at the cast on her ankle as her entire tennis career played out across the stage of her mind. Without tennis, who was she, really? A washed-up has-been. A nobody. How could this possibly be what God created her to be?

❧

Cam paused in the atrium entrance, his heart thudding at the sight of Jilly's forlorn expression. He glanced at the tray of drinks he carried and considered ducking down the corridor to give Jilly and Alice a few more minutes alone.

Then Alice caught his eye and signaled him over. Disguising his concern with a casual grin, he sauntered in and set the drink tray on a glass-top coffee table. "Cranberry juice for the ladies and a decaf for me."

"Why, thank you, Cam." Alice winked. "I hope you didn't get lost in the maze of hallways."

"Nope. Thought I'd take the scenic route." He perched

on the edge of a chair across from them. Passing them their drinks, he cast Jilly a questioning look.

She quirked one corner of her mouth and shrugged before taking a sip of juice.

Alice tipped her head in Jilly's direction. "Our girl's a wee bit perplexed about what the future holds."

Cam had a few ideas of his own about Jilly's future. It took all his willpower not to claim her in his arms right now and tell her so. Instead, he scooted deeper into the chair and wrapped his hands around the warm cardboard sleeve of his coffee cup. "I could give you that trite saying about how we don't know what the future holds, but we can trust the One who holds our future—"

Jilly thrust out a hand. "I know, I know. And I'm trying to trust God. But if I can't play tennis again—"

"You'll find something else to do with your life. God won't leave you stranded."

"Cam knows what he's talking about, honey." Alice set her juice cup on the table, the corners of her eyes crinkling in a sad smile. "He was lost once, too."

The old regrets edged closer. Cam clenched his jaw against the sting of guilt and grief. If he wasn't careful he'd crush the coffee cup between his fists.

A soft murmur penetrated his thoughts—Jilly's voice.

"I think I have it bad because I might have to give up tennis. I can't even imagine losing a brother. How did you ever find your way after Terrance died?"

Cam's chest collapsed on a pained sigh. How could he reply, when he still groped for answers, for peace, for healing? Despite all his seminary studies, prayer retreats, and God-talk, he still fought to believe in Christ's love and forgiveness. But he *had* to believe. Most days, faith was the only thing that kept him going.

Dear Jesus, help me. I don't want to be a fraud any longer.

A favorite scripture passage from Jeremiah nudged its way

into his thoughts. *"Because of the LORD's great love we are not consumed, for his compassions never fail. They are new every morning; great is your faithfulness."*

If he had any hope of encouraging Jilly through the difficult decisions she faced—if he nurtured even the smallest hope of sharing a future with her—he'd have to dive headfirst into the Lord. He'd have to claim the compassion of Christ for himself and live in it.

&

What a week! Cam couldn't believe it was Thursday already. Unsure how long he could convince Jilly to stay in Blossom Hills once her ankle was better, he'd planned special outings with her every day. He figured the more time they spent together, the quicker she'd see they were meant for each other. Then maybe she'd forget all about returning to Modesto and decide life was pretty good right here.

After they'd said good-bye to Alice on Monday, Cam had convinced Jilly to swallow her pride and let him push her in the wheelchair along the sidewalks of Blossom Hills's quaint downtown area. Window boxes of cascading petunias graced storefronts. Several old-timers had their usual checkers tournament going in front of Max's Barbershop. A sidewalk sale at the neighborhood bookstore had Cam and Jilly sharing laughs over titles long out of print and horribly out of date.

On Tuesday Cam arranged a picnic lunch at a picturesque park, and on Wednesday they took a drive through the Ozarks. During one of their many conversations about their personal likes and dislikes, Jilly shyly revealed that ever since they'd watched *Braveheart* together all those many years ago, Mel Gibson had become her favorite actor.

So on Thursday morning, with his bags packed for the next prayer retreat, Cam stopped by the video store on his way to the inn and rented all the best Gibson movies in stock. As soon as he could drag Jilly away from working on inn business with Harvey, he parked her on the sofa in the lounge, popped *Forever Young* into the DVD player, and plied her with diet cola, buttered popcorn, and Heather's gourmet pizza.

By midnight they'd clutched each other's hands through *Ransom,* wept with each other through *The Patriot,* and chuckled through the animated feature *Pocahontas.*

"Enough! Enough already!" Laughing and bleary-eyed, Jilly wrestled the remote out of Cam's grip.

He pinned one of her arms and tried to grab the remote from her flailing hand. "Hey, we haven't even gotten to the Mad Max and Lethal Weapon movies."

"Oh, please! If it's possible to OD on Mel Gibson, I think we've just done it." She stuffed the remote between the sofa cushions, well out of Cam's reach. "Anyway, shouldn't you be studying for your retreat?"

"After leading three already, I'm as prepared as I'll ever be. Come on, how about one more serving of Mel before we call it a night?" Cam reached across her, one hand pawing under the cushions.

His opposite elbow jabbed her ribs. She yelped and gave him a shove. He jerked back, nearly sliding off the sofa before he caught himself. With a huff, he scooted onto the sofa, sliding in so close that his lips brushed her neck.

"Jilly. . .Jilly." His arm crept around her shoulders. His other hand caressed her face as he guided her lips to meet his.

The tender urgency of her response shot waves of heat down his limbs. She lifted a hand to his neck and wove her fingers through the hair at his nape. He shuddered, moaned, drew back. His gaze settled on hers, and he grinned. "Wow."

She grinned back, breathless. "My sentiments exactly."

fifteen

"Jillian. Hey, Jilly!"

She shook herself and focused on Harvey's face. He leaned across the front desk, one unruly eyebrow slanted toward the ceiling. "Sorry, guess I was daydreaming."

"Must'a' been a mighty good one, judging from that sappy smile you were wearing." Harvey chuckled. "How you comin' on those room assignments?"

Uncomfortably aware of the heat creeping up her neck, Jilly studied the computer screen. Okay, obviously Mr. and Mrs. Kaye would not like sharing their room with the Russo sisters. How had that happened? Nothing to do with lingering over the memory of Cam's amazing kiss last night.

Riiiiight.

And if the guy walked by the desk one more time with that come-hither look in his eyes, she would either have to put on blinders or switch to decaf for the rest of the day. One glance from Cam and her heart started dancing like Maria Sharapova setting up to return a serve.

She made the correction on the room list and hit the PRINT button. "That should do it, Harvey." A glance at her watch told her she'd finished none too soon. Cam's retreat guests would begin arriving any minute.

Harvey stepped around to Jilly's side of the counter. "How about I take over? You look like you could use a nap." He winked. "That mean ol' Cam's been running you all over the countryside and keeping you up till all hours of the night."

A nap sounded delightful, but it was true—she'd spent so much time with Cam all week that she'd fallen far behind on inn business. With Alice on the mend, Harvey had resumed many of his usual duties, but Jilly still managed most of the bookkeeping and scheduling—Alice's areas of expertise. She cringed at the thought of the unopened mail and paperwork screaming to her from the inner office.

On the other hand, as brainless as she felt right now, she would be risking the inn's financial ruin if she got anywhere near the accounts.

She swiveled on the barstool and reached for her walker. "Think I'll take you up on that offer, Harvey—"

The glass door to the deck whooshed open and Cam sauntered into the lobby. "Ralph's got the fire pit fueled and ready." His gaze skated past Harvey and settled on Jilly. One corner of his mouth lifted in a provocative smile. "The sky's clear as a bell. It's going to be a gorgeous night."

A gorgeous night in the company of nine retreat guests while she fought the urge to drag Cam behind the garage and drink up more of his delicious kisses? This weekend might prove to be the longest three days of her life.

❧

Cam felt as if he'd just struggled through the longest weekend of his life. The latest prayer retreat had been geared toward Sunday-school teachers and youth sponsors, so between sessions and late into the evening he found himself cornered with questions about practical application. Usually he thrived on digging deeper into theology and helping others expand their understanding. But when he'd planned the content and direction of these retreats, he never anticipated the distraction of falling deeper and deeper in love.

Much less having the object of his affection close enough to set his insides aflame every time he walked through the lobby.

By the time the last participant left on Sunday afternoon, Cam caved beneath the physical and mental exhaustion. He found Jilly in the office. After buzzing her cheek with a lazy kiss, he plopped into the chair next to the desk.

She nailed him with a doubtful smirk. "Is that the best you can do?"

"Give me a five-minute nap and I'll show you."

"Promises, promises." She returned to her paperwork with a one-shoulder shrug. "From the looks of you, I don't think five minutes is quite going to handle it."

"Okay, ten. Twenty, tops." He slid lower in the chair. Legs extended, hands folded across his abdomen, he faked a chest-rattling snore.

"Terrific. If that's what you sound like when you sleep, I pity your future wife."

Cam's pulse stammered. He slitted his eyes and lifted his head an inch. "Oh, yeah? And what if I'm look—"

The ringing phone cut him off. And none too soon, considering the mixture of panic and embarrassment he'd just observed dancing across Jilly's face. He used the armrests to push himself upright as she grabbed up the receiver.

"Paul, hi! How's it going?"

They talked for a few minutes, then Jilly covered the mouthpiece and whispered to Cam, "He's doing great. They said he could move to outpatient status."

After only one week in rehab, that was good news indeed.

Except it probably meant Paul would be back at the inn. Just a friend or not, Cam wasn't so sure he liked the idea of another eligible—and actually fairly good-looking—bachelor on the premises.

Jilly finished the call and turned toward Cam. "The drugs are out of Paul's system and he's determined to keep it that way." Her lips flattened. She tapped a pen on the desk. "There's just one small stipulation about releasing him."

A prickly sensation worked its way up Cam's spine. Why did he have the feeling he wasn't going to like what she said next? "And that would be. . .?"

"He's still going to need to see his counselor every day, so he really needs a place to stay in town."

"Oh. Then we need to find him a cheap apartment or hotel near the center."

"Um, not exactly." Jilly's breath whistled through her clenched teeth. "Paul's counselor won't release him unless he has someone to stay with. Someone to help keep him accountable."

The picture became clear. Cam straightened and crossed his arms. "I'm not exactly in the market for a housemate. Maybe it would be better for Paul to stay at the center awhile longer."

"They need his bed for someone with problems a lot worse than his. And anyway, you said you're friends with his counselor."

"Ed. Yeah."

"Would he okay something not in the best interests of his patient?"

Cam cringed. She had him there. Still, he hadn't counted on stepping in as accountability coach for a virtual stranger.

On the other hand, with Paul staying in town, Cam would have fewer worries about any possible rivalry for Jilly's affections.

He raised his hands, palms outward. "Okay, okay. I just hope he likes cats."

"Oh, thank you, thank you, thank you!" Jilly shoved herself out of the chair, spun on one foot, and landed on his lap. She threw her arms around his neck and pressed her cheek against his.

Suddenly he forgot all about that nap he'd been so sure he needed.

❧

The pungent odor of fish swirled around Cam's head as he dumped a can of tuna-mackerel mush into Bart's food dish. Before he drove over to the New Life Center to pick up Paul this morning, he'd better take another swipe at the litter box. Cats certainly made for very *aromatic* pets.

He'd started out back with a plastic bag of soiled litter when the doorbell rang. Great. The last time he had an unexpected visitor, he found Liz on his doorstep. Surely she hadn't come to ply more of her futile charm tactics?

The chiming became insistent. "Okay, I'm coming."

But not with this smelly bag of cat litter. Cam yanked open the patio door and tossed the bag behind a potted plant, then decided he should probably wash his hands before greeting whoever seemed so anxious to see him this early on a Monday morning.

Finally he made it to the front door, his hands still dripping. "Jilly. Harvey. What are you two doing here?"

Jilly huffed. "That's a real friendly greeting. Can we come in before my one good leg goes numb from standing on it so long?"

"Yeah, sure." Dumbfounded, Cam made room for Jilly and her walker to pass.

Harvey wiped his feet on the doormat. "Sorry if we took you by surprise. Jillian really wanted to go with you to get Paul, and since I was coming to town to visit Alice, I offered to drop her off here."

Jilly headed for the bench next to the coat tree and sank down with a groan. "This cast cannot come off soon enough— oh, hi, kitty. You must be the infamous Bart."

Cam rushed over and swooped the old cat into his arms. "Hey, your allergies—should you even be inside my house?"

"It's okay, let me hold him. Cat dander is among the few things on earth I am *not* allergic to." She grinned. "Otherwise, as a cat owner you'd never have gotten within ten feet of me before my eyes swelled shut."

A welcome wave of relief surged through Cam. If it came down to a choice between Bart and Jilly. . .well, there was no choice. But he hesitated to think how painful it would have been if he had to find another home for Bart.

Jilly held out her arms and took the cat onto her lap. Bart's purring soon filled the entryway. "Wow, I think he likes me."

Cam knelt beside Jilly and smiled up at her. "What's not to like?"

"Oh, brother." Harvey heaved an exaggerated groan. "It's getting too deep in here for me. I'm off to see Alice. You two lovebirds stay out of trouble, you hear?"

Cam hardly glanced up as the door closed behind Harvey.

❧

"Um, maybe we ought to think about heading over to the rehab center." Jilly had long since forsaken the purring cat. Cupping Cam's face between her palms to savor his kisses was much more enjoyable. Except it was getting awfully hot in this tiny entryway.

Still kneeling, Cam shifted his weight to his heels. "Yeah, Harvey did tell us to stay out of trouble. And I'm gonna be in big trouble if you keep kissing me like that."

Jilly shook a finger in Cam's face. "Why, Mr. Lane, don't you dare put all the blame on me. If you weren't so incredibly handsome—"

"Please!" Cam thrust to his feet and pulled Jilly up with one hand while moving her walker closer with the other. "Let's go get Paul while I still have any willpower left."

The Paul who greeted them in the New Life waiting room looked light-years healthier than he had one week ago when they brought him in. His year-round tennis tan had faded slightly, but his eyes seemed brighter, his posture more erect.

Jilly scooted closer and wrapped him in a hug. "It's so good to see you looking like your old self again."

"Feels good, too. Thanks for coming to get me." Paul stepped back and nodded at Cam. "And thanks for giving me a place to stay, man."

"No prob." Cam shuffled closer, extending his right hand to shake Paul's. His other arm settled firmly around Jilly's shoulders—almost possessively if she were to hazard an opinion.

A shiver zinged through her. Things with Cam had moved at lightning speed this past week. She'd relished every moment of their time together, but if she allowed herself to fall any more in love with the guy, she could never bear to leave him. Modesto—or wherever her tennis career took her—would be too far away.

Her ankle cast suddenly dragged her leg down like a lead weight. *You keep forgetting, Gardner. Your tennis career could very well be history.*

"Jilly?"

She looked up to see Cam frowning at her, a worried look creasing his brow. "Sorry, just frustrated with this cast and walker. Paul, you ready to go?"

Back at Cam's house, Jilly made herself comfortable on the den sofa while Cam showed Paul to the guest room and helped him settle in. Cam's Bible lay on the end table, a devotion booklet beside it open to today's date. Cam must have been sitting in this very spot for his morning Bible study. Even hours later, Jilly imagined the plush ribbed velour still held the warmth from his body. Her eyes drifted shut for a moment. A yearning sigh escaped her lips.

Looking toward the front door, she glimpsed the bench by the coat rack, and immediately her lips tingled with the memory of Cam's kisses. There was so much to love about him. His tenderness. His faith. His generosity. She had the feeling she could ask anything of Cam and he'd go to the ends of the earth to please her.

But, if by God's grace, Jilly made it back on the tennis circuit—something she prayed for with all her heart—how could she ask Cam to come with her? To leave behind his home, his church, his professorship at Rehoboth Bible College?

Oh, Lord, I love him so. Don't make it a choice between Cam and my career.

Once again, her glance drifted to the Bible. She drew the weighty, leather-covered volume onto her lap and let the onion-skin pages fall open in the New Testament. Her gaze skimmed the verses for any perceived word from the Lord, until she found herself in the book of Philippians. Here, Cam had highlighted chapter 4, verse 6: "Do not be anxious about anything, but in everything, by prayer and petition, with thanksgiving, present your requests to God."

Anxious. She'd been plenty anxious lately. About her career. About her relationship with Harvey and Alice. About Paul and the steroid scandal.

And most of all, about the possibility of a future with Cam. *Jesus, I'm trying to pray, trying to turn all this over to You.*

A furry head nudged beneath Jilly's elbow. Bart must have grown bored trailing Cam and Paul on the house tour. Jilly ran her hand down the length of the cat's arching back, static electricity raising Bart's hair all the way down to his tail. He showed his appreciation with a noisy purr.

"Doesn't take much to make you happy, huh, fella?" Oh, for the simple life of a house cat.

Footsteps drifted from the hallway. Sliding the Bible onto the end table, Jilly looked up to see Cam striding toward her. "Did you get Paul moved in?"

"We rearranged some things in the closet and bathroom to give him some space." Cam crossed in front of her and opened the back door. "It's a gorgeous day. How about sandwiches on the patio?"

"Is it lunchtime already? I can help." Reaching for her walker, she pulled herself off the sofa.

"I can handle it. You go on outside." With scarcely a glance in her direction, Cam bustled to the kitchen.

Obviously with Paul in the house, Cam must be playing it cool. She knew as well as he did that if he dared get too close, they'd be in each other's arms in a matter of seconds. Okay, she'd play along. . .for now. She shuffled out the door and chose a padded swivel chair in the shade of the patio table umbrella.

Seconds later a putrid odor assaulted her nostrils. She wrinkled her nose. "Eeew! Hey, Cam, it smells like something died out here."

Cam darted out. "Oops. Forget about the cat litter. I'll run it out to the trash can."

"Please do." Jilly frowned at the cat, who had followed Cam and now wound through the legs of her walker. "Whoa, buddy, you are some stink machine."

Somewhere in the neighborhood a lawn mower rumbled. The breeze carried the scent of exhaust fumes and grass clippings. Jilly sneezed. And sneezed again. "Oh boy."

Digging a tissue out of her jeans pocket, she glimpsed Cam loping across the lawn. He stepped onto the patio as a third sneeze doubled her over. "You okay?"

"I'm late taking my allergy pill this morning. The bottle's in my purse. Would you mind bringing it to me with a glass of water?"

"Sure, right away."

On second thought, maybe she should go inside and stay there until the medication kicked in. Between sneezes she worked her way through the door, and in one motion shoved the walker aside and dropped onto the sofa cushions.

Cam rushed over with a glass of water and her pill bottle. "Guess fresh air wasn't such a good idea after all."

She sniffled as Cam shook a pill into her open palm. "My fault. I was supposed to take my pill at ten, and we got so busy with. . .other things. . .that I forgot."

He grinned knowingly as he capped the bottle and dropped it into her purse. "Next time remind me and I'll set a timer."

The pill slid down on a sip of water, and she rested her head on the back of the sofa. "I'll be okay in a few minutes."

"I'm in the kitchen making sandwiches. Holler if you need anything else."

She nodded and closed her eyes.

Minutes later she jerked upright. Something didn't feel right. Her chest hurt, as if the pill had gotten stuck on the way down. She swallowed the rising saliva and waited for the sensation to pass, but it only grew worse.

The roof of her mouth began to itch. Her lips tingled—and this time not pleasantly. Heat flamed up her chest, her neck, her face. She tried to cough, but it came out in a painful wheeze.

"Jilly?" Cam rushed from the kitchen. He leaned over her, one hand on her back. "Jilly!"

His voice sounded far away. A misty curtain slid over her eyes. Her head tipped backward. Her last conscious thought was that Cam really ought to paint that water stain on his ceiling.

❧

"Jilly. Jilly!" Cam eased her sideways onto the sofa while his panicked brain tried to make sense of the situation. You couldn't pass out from sneezing, could you? At least she was breathing—but like Darth Vader with a chest cold. "Jilly, can you hear me?"

God, what's happening here?

"Cam? Is everyth—" Paul skidded to a halt beside him. "Oh, man. This isn't good." He dropped on one knee and checked Jilly's pulse and airway. "Hang on, girl. Keep breathing."

Her eyes fluttered open. She groped for Paul's hand, her chest heaving with every grating breath.

"Do you know what's wrong with her?" Cam didn't recognize his own voice. And he barely recognized the woman lying on the sofa, her face ashen, her lips a hideous shade of blue. An angry rash mottled the skin around her mouth.

"Looks like anaphylactic shock. Where's her purse? She always carries an epinephrine injection."

"It's, uh—" Cam's mouth tasted like old pennies. He stood. Backed away. Clawed his hair. *Please, God, help her!*

Paul shot him an impatient glare. "Find her purse, man! And call 911."

Cam forced himself to swallow, to think. His gaze scoured the room until it fell upon Jilly's purse. He grabbed it and thrust it at Paul, then stumbled to the kitchen phone. While he explained Jilly's condition to the operator, he watched Paul snap open a tube-like container and jab it into Jilly's thigh, then massage the area roughly.

Even from the kitchen, Cam could hear the change in Jilly's breathing. The rhythm steadied, the sound grew less labored and raspy. Phone receiver cradled in his hands, he sank into the nearest chair and waited for the thudding of his own heart to subside.

As the wail of sirens neared, one thought pounded through Cam's brain: *You froze, man. When she needed you the most, you froze.*

sixteen

"I don't understand." Jilly had to force the words out over her raspy throat. She drew both hands through the hair at her temples and plopped her head against the mushy hospital pillow. "The only thing I react to that way is macadamia nuts. And I wasn't anywhere near nuts today."

The ER doctor checked her bedside monitor and jotted something on his clipboard. "What were you doing just before this happened?"

Jilly gave a hoarse laugh. "Taking my allergy pill."

"Do you have the pills with you?"

"They were in my purse, but. . ." She glanced over at Paul, who sat stiffly on a hard plastic chair.

"Your purse must still be at Cam's." Paul stood. "You want me to call him?"

A sick feeling churned through Jilly's stomach. Her mind locked on the image of Cam standing on his front porch as the EMTs wheeled her down the sidewalk to the ambulance. The anxious little-boy look on his face shredded her heart.

"Jilly?" Paul's soft reminder drew her attention.

She frowned at the doctor. "Do you really need to see the pills?"

"If that was the last thing you ingested, yes. We need to determine exactly what precipitated the anaphylaxis."

Paul sidled toward the opening in the privacy curtain. "I'll step out and call Cam. Be right back."

The doctor finished his exam and excused himself, leaving Jilly alone in the brightly lit cubicle. She stared at four and a half pale, wrinkled toes protruding from the ankle cast that had become the bane of her existence. "If not for you, you stupid thing, I'd still be in Modesto. I'd still have a job. I'd still have hopes of making it to the US Open. . . . Okay, so, maybe not. But I wouldn't be sitting here in a hospital bed, mooning over a guy with issues of his own."

"Talking to yourself?" Paul ducked through the curtain. "Not a good sign."

Jilly sniffed back tears that threatened to clog the plastic tubes feeding her oxygen. Good grief, she'd turned into a veritable fountain lately. "Did you reach Cam?"

"He's bringing your purse." Paul nudged his chair closer to the stretcher and plopped down. "What's the deal with him anyway? I thought he'd want to come with you to the hospital."

Jilly mashed her lips together to suppress a shudder. "When he gets here, don't be too hard on him, okay?"

"If you say so." Paul leaned back and crossed his arms. "He sure freaked, though. For a minute there, I was afraid I'd be scraping him off the floor."

"Seeing me like that, thinking I might be dying. . .it must have really scared him."

"Yeah, you told me about his brother. Losing someone you care so much about. . .I guess it's something you never completely get over."

"Anyway, have I thanked you for remembering my epinephrine?" She reached for Paul's hand. "You probably did save my life."

Paul screwed his mouth into a bashful grin. "Aw, shucks, ma'am, weren't nothin'."

An amazon of a nurse came in to take Jilly's vitals and check her IV. Before she finished, an aide appeared with Jilly's purse and set it in her lap. "A gentleman just left this for you at the desk."

Jilly's heart rate soared. She sat forward and tried to see past the aide through the slit in the curtain. "Is he still here?"

"Take it easy, ma'am. Breathe normally and relax." The

nurse, in the middle of taking a blood pressure reading, poked a meaty fingertip to Jilly's breastbone and nudged her back against the pillow.

Jilly shot Paul a pleading gaze. He nodded and left the cubicle, only to return moments later to say Cam had already left. Jilly sagged under the weight of disappointment and quietly let the nurse finish her exam. Part of her sympathized with Cam's terror, but couldn't he at least look in on her to make sure she was all right?

Paul touched her arm. "Jilly, your pills. The doctor's waiting for them."

"Oh, right." Giving herself a mental shake, Jilly unzipped her purse and retrieved the vial of allergy pills. She shoved it into the nurse's outstretched hand. "I don't know what they expect to find. I've been taking this same prescription for three or four years now."

&

After handing over Jilly's purse to an attendant at the ER desk, Cam wasted no time escaping the cloying hospital atmosphere. Five steps out the sliding glass doors, he zigged left and collapsed against a pillar. Across from him purple and red petunias overflowing a concrete planter mocked him with their cheerfulness.

Shame crawled through him like an ugly spider. What a coward! What a helpless, useless mass of nerves. If Paul hadn't been there—*Oh God!* It didn't bear thinking about.

But you didn't lose her. She's okay. And you're out here feeling sorry for yourself while she's in there probably wondering what kind of idiot professes his love and then chokes in a crisis.

For better or for worse? Oops, flubbed that one already. Good thing they were still a long way from the proposal stage.

Cam hauled in a shuddering breath. Time to buck up and be a man. He owed Jilly—and Paul—an apology.

The glass doors glided open, and Cam strode to the admitting desk. The same woman he'd handed Jilly's purse to looked up from her computer terminal. "Something else I can do for you, sir?"

"Can I see her? Jilly Gardner?"

"Are you family?"

"No, but—"

"Then I'm sorry, I can't help you."

Frustration deflated Cam's lungs. "Could you at least let her know I'm here?"

"Name, please?"

"Cam Lane."

The woman nodded to a silver-haired aide in a lavender smock. The aide disappeared down a corridor, and Cam stepped to one side.

Behind the desk, a doctor settled in at one of the work areas and began scrawling notes in a file. A tall, heavyset nurse approached and handed the doctor a pill bottle. "Miss Gardner found her prescription. Do you want me to send it down to the lab?"

At the mention of Jilly's name, Cam edged closer. The doctor took the vial and studied the label. One eyebrow lifted. "Hmmm, one of the more potent allergy meds, but I've never heard of it causing anaphylaxis." He uncapped the vial and peered inside. "There's some kind of powdery residue. That's not normal for this drug either. Yeah, send it down to the lab and have them put a rush on the results."

A tap on Cam's shoulder made him jump. He whirled around to see the aide in the lavender smock smiling up at him. "Miss Gardner wants to see you. I'll show you the way."

He hesitated. His first impulse was to snag that doctor and find out exactly what the guy thought was wrong with Jilly's pills. Before he could react, the doctor grabbed up another file and headed off in a different direction. Cam reined in his urgent need for answers and followed the aide down a corridor reeking of disinfectant and other smells he'd just as soon not identify. The aide peeled back a curtain to reveal Jilly gazing at him through shimmering eyes.

A sudden attack of shyness curbed his headlong rush to her side. He stopped at the foot of the stretcher. "Wow, you sure look better than the last time I saw you."

One side of her mouth curled up. "I could say the same for you."

Paul stood and edged past Cam. "Think I'll go find a coffee machine."

Without taking his eyes off Jilly, Cam tipped his head toward Paul. "Take your time."

Through the thin curtain, muted voices joined the squeak of rubber-soled footsteps and rattling wheels. Ignoring everything but the woman before him, Cam stepped to Jilly's side and took her hand. His glance fell to their clasped fingers. "Can you forgive me for abandoning you? I was just so scared."

"It's okay. I understand." She tugged him closer. "So quit apologizing and kiss me."

❧

Jilly angled an irritated glance at the nurse checking her blood pressure for what felt like the millionth time in the past three hours. "I'm feeling fine. Are they ever going to let me out of here?"

"Dr. Hayes won't release you until your heart rate, BP, and oxygen levels normalize. He's also waiting on confirmation from the lab about what brought on the anaphylaxis."

"Speaking of which. . ." The doctor breezed through the curtain, clipboard in hand.

Both Cam and Paul rose and stood next to Jilly, their eagerness for answers as palpable as her own. Cam spoke first. "What did you find, Doctor? Was it the pills?"

"The pills themselves are fine. But the lab found traces of macadamia nut powder in the vial and coating several of the pills."

Jilly's stomach somersaulted. "That's insane! How could

my pills be contaminated with macadamia nuts?"

"I hate to even suggest this." Dr. Hayes's mouth spread into a grimace. "Is there anyone who would want to harm you—someone who knows about your allergy?"

She looked from Cam to Paul, her thoughts racing. "There was some trouble back in Modesto. In fact, I'm suspicious the fall that broke my ankle was no accident."

"She's right, Doc." Paul shoved his hands in his pockets. "A couple of guys on our country club tennis team were dealing steroids and thought Jilly might be on to them."

Jilly's mind flashed to the damaged packaging of her mail-order prescription. She explained what her landlady had told her and how the package was so late in showing up. "But still, how would any of those kids have known about my allergy?"

Paul grimaced. "Remember the Christmas party? I sent the boys to the bakery for cookies. And I specifically told them nothing with macadamia nuts because you were allergic."

The doctor checked his notes. "This happened in Modesto? But the vial you gave me had a Riley's Pharmacy label. That's right here in Blossom Hills."

At Cam's sudden intake of breath, Jilly swung her gaze toward him. "Oh, Cam, don't jump to conclusions. The Riley's prescription was only a couple of weeks' worth, so I topped it off with the mail-order pills and put the bigger bottle away for now."

"Without examining the other vial, we won't know which prescription is the actual source of the contamination." Dr. Hayes narrowed his gaze. "Miss Gardner, I strongly suggest you notify the police and let them conduct a full investigation. I don't think I have to tell you how serious this could have been if your friend hadn't injected the epinephrine so quickly."

Again she felt Cam cringe. She gripped his hand. "Okay, Doc, we get it. Will you release me now?"

❧

Later that evening, as they turned onto Cam's street, Jilly

glimpsed Harvey's truck parked in front of Cam's house. She sucked in her breath. "Oh no, did anyone think to let Harvey know what's going on?"

"I phoned him as soon as I knew you were okay." Cam hit the remote on his visor and waited for the garage door to open, then drove inside.

Harvey bustled through the kitchen door, ready to help Jilly out of the SUV. "Honey, honey! Thank the Lord you're all right."

"I'm fine, I promise." Leaning on Harvey's arm, Jilly hobbled up the single step into the house, where Paul had already moved her walker. She maneuvered to a kitchen chair and plopped down, more from relief than exhaustion. Three emergency trips to the hospital in the space of one month seemed a bit excessive.

The doorbell rang. Cam tossed his keys onto the kitchen counter. "Maybe that's Ralph."

"Ralph?" Harvey shifted his confused expression to Cam. "What's he doing here this late?"

As Cam headed for the door, Jilly said, "I called him. I needed him to bring something from the inn." She laid a hand on Harvey's arm. "Maybe you'd better sit down."

By the time Cam ushered Ralph into the kitchen, Jilly had explained about the contaminated prescription. Ralph dropped a brown paper grocery sack onto the table. "Found the packaging in your bathroom wastebasket, just like you said, Jilly. Got your bottle of pills, too."

"Thanks, Ralph." Jilly spread open the top of the bag and peered inside.

The doorbell chimed again. Cam pivoted. "And that'll be Keith Nelson."

Harvey gasped. "Oh, my goodness, you called Keith?"

"Cam said he's the best." Jilly couldn't help but smile at the thought of seeing her almost-cousin again, a hot-tempered rookie on the Blossom Hills police force last time she saw him. She was pleasantly surprised when Cam told her Keith Nelson had matured into one of the sharpest detectives in the state.

Harvey slid a hand down his face and fell into the chair next to Jilly. "You really think this was deliberate? That someone intended to harm you, possibly even kill you?"

She'd had several hours to process the idea, but it still turned her insides to jelly. And when she glimpsed the solemn expression in Detective Keith Nelson's deep blue eyes, her mouth went too dry to speak.

❧

Cam braced one hip against the kitchen counter and listened in silence as Jilly and Paul gave Keith a detailed account of all the events leading up to today. His mind, however, spun out prayer after prayer that the investigation would clear Liz—for her and Sammy's sake as well as for Cam's peace of mind.

"Okay, I think I've got this all straight." Keith flipped his notebook shut and rose. "But I'm telling you, Jilly, next time you show up in town without calling me for a lunch date, I'll have no choice but to run you in for failure to appear."

She smirked. "Between Harvey and Cam, I've been staying pretty busy since I came home."

Keith extended his hand to Cam. "Good to see you again, man. Take care of this gal, you hear me? You, too, Uncle Harvey. Give my love to Aunt Alice, and tell her I'll try to get by to see her in a few days."

"Sure will, son." Harvey stood and walked Keith to the door.

Twenty minutes after Keith left, Cam had his duffel bag restocked with clean clothes for a return trip to the inn. No way was he letting Jilly out of his sight until the police got this mess straightened out. Planning to ride out with Harvey and Jilly, he gave Paul the keys to his house and car, along with instructions for looking after Bart—although Paul didn't look real keen on the litter box business.

"Look, you need to stay in town for your rehab sessions. I'll check in with you every chance I get, and I also asked my pastor to stop by. You've got Ed's number at the center and my cell if you need any help." Cam waited until Harvey and Jilly had started out to the pickup before continuing. "Besides, we both need to be sure nothing else happens to Jilly."

Paul rammed his fingers into his back pockets. "I hate this, man. If one of my kids did this to her—"

Cam left his own thoughts unspoken. His mind kept returning to the Riley's prescription bottle. . .and Liz. She'd been furious the day they broke up, but angry enough to hurt someone? The mere idea made his stomach cramp. No, Liz was a good woman, a devoted mother. Besides, how would she have known about Jilly's macadamia nut allergy? Cam hadn't even been aware of it until today.

Paul nudged his arm. "Better get moving or they'll leave without you."

"Yeah." Cam looked toward the door as a fresh wave of doubt assailed him. He'd do everything in his power to keep Jilly safe until the police nailed the culprit. But he wouldn't—couldn't—put his own heart on the line again.

Sorry, God, not even what little faith I have would be enough to get me through losing Jilly.

seventeen

Jilly looked up from the mail she'd been sorting and heaved a sigh. Across the lobby, Cam sat on a love seat facing away from her, apparently engrossed in some heavy reading. He'd barely spoken five words to her all morning. In fact, ever since they'd arrived at the inn yesterday, he'd hardly even made eye contact. And when he did, his expression revealed nothing. It was as if the man she'd begun to fall in love with had disappeared, leaving only a shell.

The front door swung open, setting off a chime. Cam tossed his book aside and lunged to his feet, waylaying Keith Nelson before he made it through the door. "Did you get the lab results? Do you know who did this?"

"Give the poor man some breathing room, Cam." Jilly maneuvered her walker around the front desk and scooted over to the seating area. "What is it, Keith? Did you find out anything?"

"I've got a few answers for you." Keith's face was all business. He tugged a notebook from the inside pocket of his navy blazer. "The prescription sent from Modesto is definitely the source of the contamination. The lab found macadamia nut powder not only inside the prescription vial but in minute traces under the tape used to reseal the original packaging."

"Then it must have been one of the kids dealing steroids. They stole it off my porch." Jilly sank into the nearest chair, not sure whether to feel relieved or even more terrified. She glanced up at Cam. His head fell forward. He covered his eyes with one hand before turning away.

Keith took the chair opposite Jilly and braced his elbows on his thighs. "I've been in touch with the investigating officer in

148

the steroid case, and I'm forwarding all the evidence and lab reports directly to the Modesto Police Department."

Cam stepped closer, fists knotted at his sides. "Did you find any fingerprints? DNA? *Anything* you can use to nail these creeps to the wall?"

At the jagged edge in Cam's tone, Jilly cringed. She'd never seen him so angry.

Keith closed his notebook and shrugged. "We did find a partial print under the sealing tape, but it didn't have enough detail to match with prints on file."

"That's just great." Cam thrust one hand to the back of his neck. "For lack of solid evidence some street-smart dopehead could get away with attempted murder."

"I didn't say that, Cam." Keith's professional calm belied the concern Jilly read behind his eyes. "Now that the Modesto cops know what they're looking for, they'll be checking the suspects' homes, cars, and clothing for any trace of the contaminant."

Jilly cupped her palms around her temples. "So what happens next, Keith?"

"More than likely, you'll have to go back to Modesto to give statements and ID the suspects. You should be hearing from. . ." He consulted his notebook. "Detective Leigh Smith. She can fill you in on where the case stands and answer any questions about what will be expected of you."

"Wow, what a summer. I feel like I've been on a never-ending roller-coaster ride." Jilly shot a quick glance toward Cam, who stood with his back to them in the lounge doorway. What was still eating him? Shouldn't he be relieved to know the crime originated in Modesto, not the Blossom Hills pharmacy he'd suggested?

Keith pushed up from the chair. "I need to get back to town. But remember, I'm only a phone call away if you need anything."

Jilly pulled up on her walker and stretched to wrap an arm

around Keith's neck. "Thanks, Keith. I'm sure glad we had you on this case."

"Glad I could help." He nodded in Cam's direction and lowered his voice. "Hang in there with him. He's scared, that's all. He'll come around."

"I hope you're right."

※

Three days later, Ralph drove Jilly and Paul to the Kansas City airport. Though Detective Smith already had Paul's statement and had cleared him of any related charges, Paul was itching to return home and—if Therese would still have him—get back to work. His rehab counselor set up a referral to a Modesto facility so that Paul's recovery could continue uninterrupted.

Watching the Ozarks fade to shades of purple along the eastern horizon, Jilly sent up a silent prayer of thanks for Paul's amazing turnaround. Now, she could only pray Cam would come to his senses. Guilt over missing the signs of Terrance's steroid abuse, combined with his fears about what *could* have happened to Jilly as a result of teens using steroids, had grown into an impenetrable wall between Cam and everyone he cared about. Not even Harvey's homegrown wisdom or Alice's prayerful prodding seemed to have any effect.

At the Sacramento airport Jilly and Paul arranged for a shuttle to take them straight to the Modesto Police Department. Detective Leigh Smith ushered them to her desk, moving a box of files out of the way to give Jilly space to maneuver. Now that her ribs were healing, she'd ditched the cumbersome walker and had gone back to using crutches.

"I appreciate your coming straight here." The detective edged behind her desk and shuffled through some files. "We've had a break in the case since last time I talked to you."

"Really? That's great." Jilly sipped from a bottle of water she'd purchased at the airport.

"Alex, one of the boys dealing steroids, decided to talk." Smith narrowed her gaze over the rim of tortoiseshell reading glasses. "He fingered his cousin, a hospital tech named Frank Ford, as the supplier."

Paul ran a hand down his face. "I knew it had to be something like that. Those kids weren't smart enough or well-connected enough to be getting the drugs on their own."

"Exactly." Smith turned toward Jilly. "Alex admitted he and his friend Ted tried to scare you into silence because *they* were scared of Ford and didn't want him to find out their little enterprise may have been compromised. Then they heard at the country club that you'd left town, so they kept an eye on your apartment, watching for your return. When your prescription was delivered, they snatched it on a whim."

Jilly's lips flattened. "What about the macadamia nut powder?"

"The boys got worried that you'd left town to protect yourself because you were planning to turn them in, so they finally told Ford everything and gave him the package they'd stolen. When Ford saw it was a prescription, he figured you'd be needing it soon and thought they could use it somehow to get to you. That's when Alex remembered your macadamia nut allergy."

"So they contaminated my pills and then left the package back at my apartment. You can prove this, right?"

"Based on Alex's statement, we obtained a search warrant for Ford's apartment. Stuffed in the back of a closet we found a trash bag with an empty nut can and a pair of latex gloves with the powder clinging to them." The detective chuckled. "That tech should really think about taking out his trash more often."

Smith went on to explain that the crime lab matched prints found inside the gloves with those of the hospital tech. When questioned, Ford was all too ready to make a deal in exchange for a list of everyone he'd been supplying drugs to.

Cold fingers tightened around Jilly's midsection. "Exactly what kind of deal?"

"We prosecute for the lesser charge of aggravated assault instead of attempted murder. After all, he can claim his intent was only to scare you, not kill you."

"Aggravated assault?" Jilly sat forward, hands clamped around the armrests. "You realize I could have died?"

The detective lowered her gaze. "Of course I do, and I don't mean to play down the seriousness of what happened to you. But Alex and Ted did eventually cooperate and, being minors, the boys will most likely do their time in the juvenile justice system—always with the hope of rehabilitation. On the other hand, even on the lesser charge, Frank Ford can expect a pretty stiff sentence."

❧

The last thing on earth Cam felt like doing this weekend was leading another prayer retreat. He drove around behind the inn, shut off the engine, and leaned his head on the steering wheel. "Lord, give me strength."

A tap on the window glass brought him up with a jolt. Harvey pulled open the door. "Thought maybe something happened to you. A couple of your retreat folks have already checked in."

"Sorry." Cam heaved himself from the SUV and retrieved his duffle bag from the backseat. "I'll go see to them right now."

"No hurry. Ralph and Heather are keeping them entertained with coffee and conversation." Harvey matched Cam's slow pace toward the deck steps. "What's wrong, son? Missing Jillian?"

Like crazy. But he couldn't let himself even think about her. He kept his response noncommittal. "You heard if they got to Modesto okay?"

"She called about twenty minutes ago. Already met with the detective." Harvey filled Cam in on the details Jilly had learned.

Relief settled across Cam's shoulders. He elbowed his way through the glass door to the lobby. "Good. Now maybe she can put this mess behind her and get on with her life."

And maybe I can, too.

Harvey sighed as he stepped behind the front desk. "Sure hope so. She's gonna have an awful hard time adjusting to life without tennis, though, if it comes to that."

Cam dropped his duffel bag and rested his forearms on the counter. "You think it will?"

"Before she left, she got the name of a top-notch Modesto orthopedist and made an appointment to see him first thing Monday." Harvey shuffled through some registration cards. "Whatever he tells her will be the deciding factor."

A whirlwind of emotions twisted through Cam's gut. If Jilly couldn't play tennis again, would she return to Blossom Hills? And if she did, how could he bear having her so close? Yet if she went back on the tennis circuit, he might never see her again. Either option meant sheer torture.

❧

Paul, Therese, and Denise had each offered to take Jilly to her orthopedist appointment, but she insisted she could drive herself. If the prognosis came back as she feared it would— and prayed it wouldn't—she'd rather not have an audience.

After several X-rays and a CT scan of her ankle, the doctor didn't keep her in suspense. "Whoever did your surgery after the second fall did everything right. But even with intensive physical therapy, you'll never regain full range of motion, and there'll always be some weakness. You'll be good for most routine activities, even an occasional recreational tennis game. But to subject that ankle to the stresses of professional tennis would be risking permanent disability."

The tears she expected didn't come. Even two hours later, sitting alone in her apartment and staring at a blank TV screen while sipping diet cola, she felt nothing more than a vague emptiness.

So she couldn't play professional tennis anymore. She still had two good legs, or would as soon as this cast came off. She had a brain. And she had a family.

Thank You, Lord, for giving me back Harvey and Alice.

Her cell phone warbled. She retrieved it from her purse and checked the caller ID. Therese.

Acceptance sat upon her shoulders like a heavy blanket. She flipped open the phone and prepared to offer her official resignation as women's tennis instructor at Silverheels Country Club.

Therese was, of course, disappointed. At least she hadn't balked at reinstating Paul, and his return helped temper the loss of Jilly.

So now what? Without her job at Silverheels, she had no reason to stay in Modesto. Decisions about her future would be a lot easier if she knew for certain Cam was waiting for her back in Blossom Hills. But he hadn't called her once since she left. And she hadn't the nerve to call him and risk his not answering, or worse, his open rejection.

"God, I'm so confused! Help me know what to do."

The act of praying spurred her to search for her Bible. Unopened for months, if not years, it lay beneath a hodge-podge of pens, pencils, old receipts, and other odds and ends in an end-table drawer. She let it fall open to where a ribbon marked the Psalms—probably placed there when the book was manufactured. Hungry for sustenance, she let her gaze slide across the verses.

Words from Psalm 62 leaped from the page: "He alone is my rock and my salvation; he is my fortress, I will not be shaken. My salvation and my honor depend on God; he is my mighty rock, my refuge."

Understanding seeped into her consciousness like a soothing cup of tea. Her life wasn't about tennis. Her life wasn't about Cam. Her life wasn't about the family she'd always felt deprived of and now cherished in Harvey and Alice.

God alone is my rock. God alone must be the source of my fulfillment and happiness.

He'd already proven He could restore lost dreams. Whatever her future held, she'd trust in the One whose love never failed.

eighteen

How he made it through another prayer retreat, Cam would never know. Okay, so he had a pretty good idea. It had to be all God, because Cam was running on empty.

Leading a group of Rehoboth Bible College students also helped a lot. All Cam had to do was throw out a discussion question and the participants took over. Nobody seemed to notice he didn't have much to say. He could only thank God it was over and pray he could get his mind in gear to prepare more thoroughly for next weekend—the final prayer retreat he'd scheduled and sure to be the most emotionally and spiritually challenging.

But first, he needed to restock his refrigerator. He steered his grocery cart along the frozen-food aisle and paused in front of a selection of microwavable dinners. Normally he took satisfaction in whipping up his own meals, but not today. He didn't want to think too hard about anything.

The open glass door quickly frosted over as he perused the shelves. Chicken teriyaki, chipotle burrito, and spinach ravioli dinners found their way into his cart. Oh, well, the spinach part had to be healthy, didn't it? Better grab a bottle of antacid on the way out.

As he turned down the next aisle, he narrowly missed ramming his cart into another shopper. "Oops, sorry—"

He sucked in his breath. *Liz.*

"Hello, Cam." Her glacial stare rivaled the ice crystals forming on his frozen dinners.

At least Sammy wasn't with her to witness this first encounter since Cam broke it off. He swallowed. His hands clenched the cart handle. "Hi, Liz. How are you?"

"Oh, just peachy." She faked a smile. "I suppose you knew the cops would question me about Jilly's prescription."

Cam flinched. "Liz, I'm sorry. I hope they didn't cause you any trouble."

"More embarrassment than anything. They said it was just routine."

"Still, I hope you know I didn't—*couldn't* believe you had anything to do with it." He stepped to the side of the shopping cart and lowered his voice. "You're a good woman, Liz. And you deserve to be happy. You and Sammy both. I'm sorry it didn't work out between us, more sorry than you can ever know."

"Get over yourself, Lane. I'm sorry, too, but I'll survive." Her eyes softened. She gave her head a small shake. "You, on the other hand, I'm not so sure about."

He drew his chin back. "What's that supposed to mean?"

"It means where romance is concerned, you've always been your own worst enemy. If you ever stop wallowing in guilt over stuff you can't control, you'll make some lucky lady a fine husband." She whipped her cart in the opposite direction, then shot him a rueful frown. "Just wish it could have been me."

Her blue-jeaned hips taunted him until she turned down the next aisle.

Her words taunted him for hours afterward. *"Your own worst enemy. . . If you ever stop wallowing in guilt. . ."*

"But I *am* guilty," he shouted as he dished up a serving of chicken liver delight for Bart. The smell warred with what should have been the tempting aroma of a spicy burrito warming in the microwave.

The old cat obviously didn't care one way or the other about Cam's guilt. *Just feed me,* he seemed to say with his incessant purring and weaving around Cam's legs. Pets had to be the quintessential example of unconditional love—or in Bart's case, unconditional indifference.

❧

"I picked up some more boxes for you." Denise edged through Jilly's apartment door with an armload of flattened cardboard packing crates. "Caught the Safeway manager before he got rid of them."

"Wow, thanks, this should be plenty." Jilly wrapped another coffee mug in newsprint and found a space for it in the box at her feet.

Denise grabbed the packing tape and reassembled one of the boxes. "Wish I could talk you into staying. Surely Modesto has way more job opportunities than Blossom Hills."

"You're probably right. But even though I love you to death"—she hooked an arm around Denise's neck and squeezed—"I need to be with my family. I've already put too much time and distance between me and the Nelsons."

"They sound like real special people." Denise smacked a kiss on Jilly's cheek before they both resumed packing. "Of course this big hurry to move to Missouri has nothing to do with that fellow you told me about."

The mention of Cam put Jilly's insides on spin cycle. More than a week had elapsed since she last saw him. He'd been standing on the deck, arms crossed in stoic silence, as Harvey helped Jilly into the pickup for the drive to the airport. A strange mixture of sadness and relief had etched frown lines around his mouth and eyes.

She glanced at the tennis racquet–shaped clock over the dinette—nine-twenty. This was Saturday, so if he followed his usual retreat schedule—which would make it eleven-twenty in Missouri—the group should be camped out in the shade of the old dogwood tree. The one she'd carved their initials into so many years ago. She'd never told him. Had he ever noticed?

Dear God, I love him so much. Help him face whatever demons haunt him. Help him find his way back to me.

❧

"Dear God, I loved her so much." Roger Tennant's voice ripped through the morning air. The poor guy couldn't be much older than Cam, but he'd lost his wife to ovarian cancer four months ago.

Cam had to bite down on the inside of his lip to stem his own surge of emotion. Though the guests on this retreat were all widows and widowers, Cam hadn't intended this to be a grief workshop. When he posted the information in the church newsletter, he'd recommended it for people who had passed at least the one-year anniversary of their spouse's death.

Apparently Roger hadn't read that far. The man's raw anguish was affecting everyone.

Ralph, a widower himself, had arranged some time off from inn duties to sit in on Cam's retreat. He laid a hand on Roger's shoulder. "It's okay, man. We've all been there. And as you can see, we all survived."

Roger looked up with brimming eyes. "How? How'd you do it? I don't even want to go on without Pamela."

Ralph looked around the circle, a slow smile creeping across his lips. "I think I can answer for everyone here. And there's only one answer: God."

Nods of agreement met his words, and Cam sent up a silent prayer of gratitude for Ralph's wisdom. The simple statement helped Cam regain a measure of control and refocus his thoughts. "I think what Ralph is saying is that when our own strength fails, when it feels like we can't survive another day, God carries us." He turned to a passage he'd marked in his Bible. "In the book of Lamentations the prophet Jeremiah writes, 'Because of the Lord's great love we are not consumed, for his compassions never fail. They are new every morning; great is your faithfulness.' Every day, all over again, we can go to God for the strength to keep living."

A shudder raked through Roger. He swiped at the wetness

on his face. "It's a good thing, because I'm all out of strength."

Cam closed the Bible. Obviously his planned agenda on prayer was out the window. Might as well go with the flow. "Maybe it would help if you shared some of your good memories of Pamela. I remember working with her on the evangelism committee a couple of years ago, but some of these people never had the chance to know her."

"Yeah. . .yeah." Roger gave a loud sniff and cleared his throat. "She was the greatest. Funny, smart, creative."

As he continued, Cam pushed himself up from the ground to ease his stiff knees while he recalled the lovely woman Roger described. The shakiness left Roger's voice. He even chuckled at some of the stories he told about his wife. And his love for her—the love they shared—resonated in every word.

Cam looked away, one hand pressed against the trunk of the dogwood tree. He squeezed his eyes shut. *Oh, God, if I could have a love like that someday!*

And then the thought hit him: *It's right in front of you, Cam. But you've got to be willing to step out in faith.*

When he opened his eyes, his breath caught. Not two inches from where his hand rested on the tree trunk, he made out a roughly carved shape. The gnarled bark had partially obscured it, but the outline of a heart was unmistakable.

And inside it, the initials JG + CL.

When the thrumming in his ears subsided, the voices of the retreat guests filtered into his consciousness.

"Wish I'd known her."

"Your Pamela was a keeper, that's for sure."

"What sweet memories. Cherish those, Roger."

And Roger's voice again: "Thanks. Just talking about her like this has made me realize it was all worth it—even the mistakes I made. I'd rather endure this pain and regret than never have loved her at all."

"Are you listening, son?"

The impression on Cam's spirit couldn't be stronger. He tilted his head heavenward and inhaled the sweet, green scents of summer. As the midday sunshine sifted through the branches and lit a fire behind his eyelids, so did God's healing touch flame in his heart. *"You made mistakes, and you will make more. But I love you anyway, and you are forgiven. Now forgive yourself, as many times as necessary. Let yourself love and be loved."*

The conversation beneath the tree had subsided. Cam glanced at his watch—noon already. He swiveled toward the group, his gaze seeking out Ralph while he snapped his cell phone off his belt. "Can you show everyone inside for lunch? I need to make a phone call."

❧

Jilly poked out her lower lip to blow a damp strand of hair off her forehead. "I had no idea I'd collected this much stuff since I moved in."

"How are you planning to get it all to Missouri?" Denise tore off a piece of tape to seal the box she'd just filled.

"It sure won't fit in my car. Guess I'll have to either rent a trailer or have it shipped." She sank onto the nearest chair and took a long swallow from her water bottle. "I need a breather. How about some lunch?"

"It's that time, isn't it? Want me to go pick something up?"

Jilly's gaze swept across the array of boxes and general packing clutter. She rasped out an exhausted moan. "I'd rather get away from this mess for a bit. Just let me freshen up."

Ten minutes later she hobbled down the apartment steps behind Denise and climbed into the passenger seat of Denise's Camry. They opted for their favorite salad buffet, Jilly's treat.

Denise speared a mandarin orange with her fork. "I sure don't envy you that long, lonesome trip. How far is it, anyway?"

"I checked online the other day. Nearly two thousand miles." Just speaking the words made Jilly weak with fatigue and dread. She sank against the seat, her fork clattering to the table.

"Oh my. That's. . ." Denise tilted her head sideways and squinted, her fork drawing invisible figures in the air. She shot Jilly a worried frown. "Honey, with a trailer, that'll be a good four days on the road."

"It's not like I have much choice." She stiffened her spine. "Hey, I'm a big girl. I'll be fine."

"You're a big girl with a broken ankle. There's no way I'm letting you take off cross-country by yourself." Denise broke into a wide grin. "Why don't you let me go with you? I can keep you company and help with the driving."

"Oh, Denise, I couldn't ask you to do that."

"Come on, it'll be fun. Besides, I've always wanted to visit Missouri."

A four-day car trip with her chatty landlady? Jilly could only imagine! And yet the idea of having a friend along on the arduous drive somehow made it more palatable. She shrugged and reached for her wheat roll. "Why not? Let's do it. Can you be ready to leave by Tuesday? Harvey's usually booked solid at the inn over the Fourth of July, so I told him I'd try to be back by the weekend so I can help."

"Shouldn't be a problem. Just need to put a hold on my mail and newspaper and get Sally next door to water my plants. Do you have your cell phone with you? I can call her right now."

Jilly unzipped her purse and fished her phone from its depths. "Give me the number and—oh, rats. The battery's dead."

nineteen

Cam snapped his cell phone closed and plunked down on a chair in the lobby. It was the afternoon break, and the retreat guests were in the lounge, savoring slices of Heather's rhubarb pie. Delicious as it surely was, Cam had lost his appetite hours ago. He'd tried Jilly's cell three times since lunch but kept getting her voice mail. Just now he'd started to leave a message but got so tongue-tied, he had to hang up before he made a total fool of himself.

He could only imagine what would go through her mind when she finally retrieved the garbled message. *Jilly? Hi, it's Cam. I, uh, wanted to tell you that. . . See, I found this thing on the tree and. . .I wondered if. . . Actually, I thought you should know—" Click.*

A hand clamped down on Cam's shoulder. He twisted to see Harvey standing above him, a questioning look in the older man's deep-set eyes. "Half your retreat folks are already upstairs in the conference room. You planning on joining them?"

"Yeah, guess I should get moving." He pushed up from the chair and started for the stairs, then pivoted. "Harvey, have you heard from Jilly recently?"

Harvey looked up from the stack of magazines he'd been arranging on an end table. "Not for a couple of days. I expect she's busy packing."

"Packing?"

"Haven't you heard?" Harvey broke into a wide grin. "She's moving back to Blossom Hills."

Electricity zinged through Cam. The best news ever for him, but it must mean Jilly's appointment with the orthopedist hadn't turned out the way she'd hoped. He sucked in a huge gulp of air and let it out slowly. "No, I hadn't heard. When do you expect her?"

"End of the week, most likely. She wants to make it back for the Fourth." Harvey tossed down a magazine and shot Cam an accusing frown. "I've been trying to keep my nose out of it, but I gotta ask. What's with you and Jilly? Up until the day she had that terrible allergic reaction, I'd have sworn things were really heating up between you. Now when we talk she'll hardly mention your name, and you've been moping around here like an abandoned puppy dog."

Cam combed his fingers through his hair and let them come to rest on the back of his neck. "I've been a little mixed up about things."

"Kinda gathered that. I've been praying for you."

"Thanks. I think it's working." Cam checked his watch. "And I'm very late for my session. If you hear from Jilly again, tell her I'm really glad she's coming home."

❧

Home. Jilly heaved a sigh as she closed the door of her garage apartment for the last time. Hard to believe in only a few days she'd once more be calling Dogwood Blossom Inn her home. With her cell phone recharged, she'd called Harvey on Sunday evening to update him about her travel plans, and as soon as she disconnected, her phone beeped with a voice mail notice—a full day after the fact, no thanks to her cellular provider. Her whole body atremble, she'd listened to Cam's bumbling message. Three times she'd almost called him back, only to decide what she had to tell him—and what she hoped and prayed he was trying to tell her—could only be said in person.

Now, if all went well, in three and a half days she'd be able to do just that.

Denise met her at the foot of the stairs. "Ready to go?"

"Ready as I'll ever be." She made her way to the rear of her Honda CRV and double-checked the hitch on the small trailer she'd rented. Even so, her belongings still jammed the backseat and cargo area almost to the roof. She slid her crutches into a gap behind the driver's seat, shoved the door closed, and climbed in behind the wheel.

Denise, already settled in the passenger seat, pumped her fist. "Road trip!"

Her now ex-landlady's enthusiasm was contagious. Jilly grinned and slipped on her sunglasses. She started the engine, plugged Denise's favorite Beach Boys CD into the stereo, and backed out of the driveway. "Blossom Hills, here we come!"

❧

Cam paced the length of the inn's front porch, pausing at the end of each trek to peer down the road. Four o'clock already and no sign of Jilly's car. Okay, so he didn't know what she drove and wouldn't recognize it anyway. It didn't help that every hour or so since noon another vehicle arrived with a family checking in for the holiday weekend.

"Cameron Lane, you are wearing a path in my porch." Alice strolled out and joined him at the railing. She'd been fluttering about the inn like a hummingbird ever since Harvey brought her home yesterday.

"I thought she'd be here by now. What time did she say they left Lincoln?"

"They were on the road by eight. Probably stopped for a long lunch. And remember, she's pulling a trailer." Alice tweaked Cam's ear. "Why you won't call her yourself is beyond me."

"I told you why." He shot her a smirk while rubbing his burning earlobe.

"Yes, and it's exactly the same reason she gave Harvey and me for why she won't call you." Alice clicked her tongue, but her eyes sparkled. "More stubborn sweethearts than you two I have never known."

"Admit it. You're loving every minute—" The low hum of a car engine rumbled through the trees. Cam's fingers tightened around the porch rail. He strained his gaze toward the bend in the road. Slanting sunlight cast a glare across the windshield of a dark blue car.

A car pulling a trailer!

"It's her!" Cam raced down the porch steps. His sneakers crunched across the gravel parking area as he ran to meet Jilly at the road.

By the time she pulled the car to a stop, his heart pounded so fiercely he thought his head would come off. His breath came in quick, noisy gasps. Every limb tingled with the anticipation of seeing her again, holding her again, kissing her again.

Then her door opened, and he froze. Took a step back. Slid trembling fingers into his back pockets.

She swung her casted ankle out of the car, then her other foot, clad in a scuffed brown driving moc. Long, tanned legs stretched upward to the hem of faded jean shorts. One hand on the door frame, the other on the steering wheel, Jilly raised her eyes to meet his.

A lazy grin spread across her mouth. "I've been stuck in this overstuffed vehicle for four days straight, and my backside is killing me. Are you just going to stand there looking goofy, or are you going to get a crowbar and pry me out of here?"

Everything around him faded into a blur. He edged forward, hands extended, reaching for the woman he loved. In one swift motion he hooked his arms under hers and pulled her to him. He sank the fingers of one hand into the thick mass of hair at her nape. With the other he pressed her closer, closer, until he felt the pounding of her heart against his own. His mouth searched out hers, and when their lips met, he tasted the salt of tears—his or Jilly's, he didn't know. He only knew he'd never let her go again.

⋰

With the sun slipping behind the hills and the stars popping out one by one, Jilly folded her hands beneath her head and peered through the branches of the old dogwood tree. Her chest rose and fell with a contented sigh.

Seated Indian-style on the blanket next to her, Cam nudged her with his knee. "Better sit up. Ralph will be starting the fireworks soon."

She traced the length of his forearm with her index finger, enjoying the feel of his taut muscle. "The only fireworks I'm interested in are happening right here under this tree."

In the gathering darkness she couldn't make out his expression, but his throaty chuckle told her all she needed to know. He eased down beside her and drew her head into the hollow of his shoulder. "Why didn't you ever tell me you carved our initials into the tree?"

"Because you were a hunky high-school kid and I was a dorky tennis jock who wasn't even on your radar."

"Not true." He kissed her forehead. "I was never hunky."

She rose up on her elbows and glared at him. "Oh, so you agree I was a dorky tennis jock? Why, you—"

A shower of blue and gold sparks exploded over the lake, followed by a concussive *pop*. From the shoreline came the oohs and aahs of Dogwood Blossom Inn's Fourth-of-July guests. Memories of other glorious Fourths here with the Nelsons propelled Jilly to the edge of the blanket for a better view.

Cam scooted next to her, one arm curling around her shoulder. She leaned into him as another explosion of light and color filled the sky. "I never thought I'd say this, but it sure is good to be home."

"Do you mean that?" Cam's warm breath tickled her ear. "I mean, you've faced a lot of changes in a really short time. Are you sure you're okay about everything?"

For a brief moment, the chill of disappointment seeped back in. "If you mean, do I have any regrets about giving up tennis, then, yeah, of course I do. But it's like I heard you say in one of your prayer retreats. God uses everything in our lives to help us grow into the person He created us to be. And through all this, God has helped me realize that tennis is something I do—or did—not who I am."

"I was thinking. I've got an idea I wanted to run by you."

She shifted to get a better look at his face, lit briefly by another burst of fireworks. "What kind of idea?"

"Remember I told you about volunteering at my church's after-school program?"

Jilly tensed. "That's how you met Liz. Tutoring her little boy, Sam."

He squeezed her shoulder and pressed his head against hers, wordless reassurance that his relationship with Liz was completely over. "We also try to get the kids involved in something fun and active, and I was thinking they might enjoy learning a little tennis."

Jilly let the idea skitter through her brain. Could she stand the daily reminder of what she'd lost? Or would it be easier if she gave up tennis entirely? "I don't know. . . ."

"I could introduce you to the program director at church next Sunday. You could meet a few of our kids." Cam's lips brushed her cheek. "You don't have to decide anything until school starts, and even then you could do it on a trial basis."

Teaching kids the sport she loved, and without the pressure of competition. The more she thought about it, the better the idea sounded. *It's all in Your hands, Lord. I'm not making any decisions tonight—*

"I was thinking something else, too." Cam's voice had grown husky. His fingertips grazed the back of Jilly's hand, sending shivers up her arm.

A tremulous breath whispered through her lips. "Wh–what were you thinking?"

"I was thinking how much I love you, Jilly Gardner. I was thinking I'd really like to make you my wife."

epilogue

Dogwood blossom time. The air pulsed with the heady scent. Four-petal white blossoms with yellow centers clustered along gnarled branches, adorning the hillside like a bride's train. Though the spring day held a chill, bright sunshine warmed the crown of Jilly's head beneath her tulle veil. Clutching a bouquet of dogwood blossoms and red roses, she smiled first at Alice, then Harvey, each walking beside her down the petal-strewn path.

Their destination: an ancient dogwood tree where a lovesick young girl once carved a heart, and inside it her initials next to those of the boy she secretly adored. JG + CL.

The boy himself—now a handsome man—watched her approach. Cam's beaming face seemed to light up the shadows cast by the tree's blossom-laden canopy. Scarcely aware of the guests who'd gathered on the lawn—Denise, Paul, Heather, Ralph, members of the Nelson clan, church friends, Cam's colleagues from Rehoboth Bible College, and Cam's parents, who'd flown in from Arizona—Jilly strode forward into the future she'd been dreaming about and planning for, ever since that night last summer under the fireworks.

The pastor smiled his welcome. "Who presents this woman to be wed?"

Harvey and Alice spoke in unison: "We, her parents, do."

Tears lodged in Jilly's throat. Harvey lifted the veil away from her face, his own eyes spilling over. She pulled the couple into her arms, love and gratitude so powerful within her that she could hardly breathe. Harvey patted her shoulder and nudged her forward, guiding her hand into Cam's. He gave their entwined fingers a squeeze, then took Alice's arm and helped her to their seats.

The rest of the ceremony went by in a blur. Jilly only knew she'd be spending the rest of her life with the man she loved. The man who completed her. The man who had helped her find her way back to God and family.

"Ladies and gentlemen, I present Mr. and Mrs. Cameron Lane." The pastor nodded at Cam. "Sir, you may kiss your bride."

"Thought you'd never ask." A twisted grin curled Cam's lips. He tugged Jilly into his arms, swooped her backward into a daring dip, and planted an earth-shattering kiss on her waiting mouth—to the whoops and applause of everyone in attendance.

"Wow!" Jilly gasped, coming up for air. "I'd say you aced that serve, Mr. Lane. I demand a rematch."

Before he could react, she whipped him around, dropped him across her bent knee, and kissed him with equal vigor. The guests cheered even louder.

Righting himself, Cam gave a whistle and grinned. "That's what I get for marrying an athlete. Everything's a competition, and she always has to win."

"And don't you forget it." Jilly edged into his arms, her tone mellowing. She spoke not just to Cam, but to everyone present. "The truth is, I've been a winner since the day my social worker told me I'd be living with the Nelsons." Her gaze sought out the only real parents she'd ever known, and she cast them a tender smile. "Harvey and Alice taught me what family, faith, and love are all about. If not for them, I wouldn't be the person I am today, and I thank God for them."

Cam kissed her again, this time slowly, deeply, gently. "And I thank God for bringing me you."

A Letter To Our Readers

Dear Reader:

In order that we might better contribute to your reading enjoyment, we would appreciate your taking a few minutes to respond to the following questions. We welcome your comments and read each form and letter we receive. When completed, please return to the following:

Fiction Editor
Heartsong Presents
PO Box 719
Uhrichsville, Ohio 44683

1. Did you enjoy reading *Where the Dogwoods Bloom* by Myra Johnson?
   ❑ Very much! I would like to see more books by this author!
   ❑ Moderately. I would have enjoyed it more if

   _____

   _____

   _____

2. Are you a member of **Heartsong Presents**? ❑ Yes ❑ No
   If no, where did you purchase this book? _____

   _____

3. How would you rate, on a scale from 1 (poor) to 5 (superior), the cover design? _____

4. On a scale from 1 (poor) to 10 (superior), please rate the following elements.

   ____ Heroine   ____ Plot
   ____ Hero   ____ Inspirational theme
   ____ Setting   ____ Secondary characters

5. These characters were special because? _____

_____

_____

6. How has this book inspired your life? _____

_____

_____

7. What settings would you like to see covered in future
   Heartsong Presents books? _____

_____

_____

8. What are some inspirational themes you would like to see
   treated in future books? ___ _____

_____

_____

9. Would you be interested in reading other **Heartsong
   Presents** titles?   ❑ Yes   ❑ No

10. Please check your age range:
   ❑ Under 18   ❑ 18-24
   ❑ 25-34   ❑ 35-45
   ❑ 46-55   ❑ Over 55

Name _____

Occupation _____

Address _____

City, State, Zip _____

E-mail _____

Simple Secrets

Gracie Temple's uncle left her a house in a rural Mennonite community. Sam Goodrich loves his fruit farm in Harmony, Kansas. Both must decide what's most important in life—before it's too late.

Contemporary, paperback, 320 pages, 5⅜" x 8"

_____

Heartsong

Presents

Great Inspirational Romance at a Great Price!

Heartsong Presents books are inspirational romances in
contemporary and historical settings, designed to give you an
enjoyable, spirit-lifting reading experience. You can choose
wonderfully written titles from some of today's best authors like
Wanda E. Brunstetter, Mary Connealy, Susan Page Davis,
Cathy Marie Hake, Joyce Livingston, and many others.

When ordering quantities less than twelve, above titles are $2.97 each.
Not all titles may be available at time of order.

HEARTSONG PRESENTS

If you love Christian romance…

$10.⁹⁹

You'll love Heartsong Presents' inspiring and faith-filled romances by today's very best Christian authors…Wanda E. Brunstetter, Mary Connealy, Susan Page Davis, Cathy Marie Hake, and Joyce Livingston, to mention a few!

When you join Heartsong Presents, you'll enjoy four brand-new, mass-market, 176-page books—two contemporary and two historical—that will build you up in your faith when you discover God's role in every relationship you read about!

Imagine…four new romances every four weeks—with men and women like you who long to meet the one God has chosen as the love of their lives…all for the low price of $10.99 postpaid.

To join, simply visit www.heartsong presents.com or complete the coupon below and mail it to the address provided.

Mass Market 176 Pages
